Nancy gripped the dashboard of the convertible and watched as the Delta Duck, a vehicle that could ride on land and in water, bounced up on the sidewalk.

"Watch me catch up to that bozo!" Joe shot the convertible forward.

"Look out!" Frank shouted. "That guy's a maniac."

Joe caught up to the Delta Duck, and the two vehicles hit a sharp downhill slope side by side. The convertible was heading straight for the Mississippi River!

Joe hit the brakes hard, but the car was going too fast to stop. At the last second, Nancy, Frank, and Joe leapt out. They hit the asphalt hard, then rolled to safety.

The Delta Duck hit the water with a splash, but instead of sinking, floated away out onto the river. Frank watched as the spy sailed away

Nancy Drew & Hardy Boys SuperMysteries

Available from ARCHWAY Paperbacks

A NANCY DREW & HARDY BOYS Super Mystery

BEST OF ENEMIES

Carolyn Keene

AN ARCHWAY PAPERBACK
Published by POCKET BOOKS
New York   London   Toronto   Sydney   Tokyo   Singapore

AN ARCHWAY PAPERBACK *Original*

An Archway Paperback published by
POCKET BOOKS, a division of Simon & Schuster Inc.
1230 Avenue of the Americas, New York, NY 10020

Copyright © 1991 by Simon & Schuster Inc.
Produced by Mega-Books of New York, Inc.

ISBN: 0-671-67465-X

First Archway Paperback printing April 1991

10 9 8 7 6 5 4 3 2

NANCY DREW, THE HARDY BOYS, AN ARCHWAY
PAPERBACK and colophon are registered trademarks of
Simon & Schuster Inc.

NANCY DREW & HARDY BOYS SUPERMYSTERY
is a trademark of Simon & Schuster Inc.

Cover art by Frank Morris

Printed in the U.S.A.

IL 7+

BEST OF ENEMIES

Chapter

One

LOOK AT THIS PLACE!" Bess Marvin exclaimed. "This is what I call style."

Nancy Drew grinned. Her friend was almost dancing across the lobby of the Peabody Hotel as she took in the beautiful decor. Nancy noticed that eighteen-year-old Bess was drawing appreciative gazes, too, from several guests. That was no surprise, she thought, admiring Bess's bright blue eyes and pretty face, framed with long blond hair.

"I wish I'd worn something dressier." Bess glanced down at her traveling outfit, an oversized sweatshirt over a short black skirt.

"Well, we can change as soon as we get to our

room," Nancy said. She was dressed in blue jeans and a summery white blouse. Also eighteen, Nancy was a slim five feet seven and had strawberry blond hair, which she'd pulled back in a ponytail.

As they approached the front desk, a tall, lean clerk leapt to attention. A tag on his jacket said his name was Tad Baker. With a hint of a southern drawl he said to the girls, "Welcome to the Memphis Peabody. The Old South at its finest."

Nancy and Bess smiled in return. "I'm Nancy Drew, and this is Bess Marvin," Nancy said. "We have reservations for a room for two."

"You sure do," Tad said. "But it didn't say here how pretty you'd be." Looking up from the computer screen at his desk, he winked flirtatiously.

Bess giggled, then tried to act serious again. Usually she loved to flirt with cute guys, but Nancy knew that Bess wasn't interested in meeting anyone new at the moment. She had recently started dating Craig Hershing, who lived back home in River Heights. Bess had spent the whole flight to Memphis talking about Craig and how much she would miss him while she was away.

Still, Tad was a good-looking guy, Nancy had to admit—blond, tanned skin, blue eyes. He had a wide, relaxed grin, with gleaming white teeth. But Nancy wasn't interested in Tad, either, as attractive as he was. Ned Nickerson, her boy-friend, would always be her one and only.

Tad handed two keys to the girls. "Your room's on the third floor, number three-eighteen. Oh, wait," he said, checking the computer screen again. "There's a message for you. It says, 'Meet us in the lobby at three forty-five.' And it's signed—"

"Frank and Joe Hardy." Nancy's blue eyes sparkled at the thought of meeting the Hardy brothers again.

"You got it. Frank and Joe Hardy. I hope you enjoy your stay here, and if you need anything, just give me a call."

Nancy and Bess followed the porter, who rolled their suitcases on a cart into the elevator and pressed the button for the third floor.

When they entered the room they had re-served, Bess said, "This is gorgeous."

Two queen-size beds were covered with blue spreads that complemented the colors of the floral-print wallpaper, and the ruffled curtains and antique furniture reminded Bess of an old country inn.

"I feel as if we're miles and miles away from River Heights," Bess said as she surveyed the view from the window.

Nancy laughed. "You *are* miles away from River Heights, Bess."

"And just think," Bess went on, "we've got

time to see everything we want to, since you're not on a case for a change."

Bess was recalling the many times she and her friend had put aside their plans to sightsee and relax when their travels had led to a mystery for Nancy to solve. She had cracked many cases in River Heights, too, and had gained the admiration of the police and townspeople for her talent at investigating crimes.

"Who's first in the shower?" Bess said.

"You go ahead," Nancy replied. "But we'd better hurry. We've got to meet Frank and Joe soon."

Like Nancy, Frank and Joe were detectives. They'd also made quite a name for themselves for solving some tough cases in their hometown of Bayport. When he'd called to ask Nancy to come along on the trip to Memphis, Frank had said their new case was no big deal. He and Joe wouldn't need help—but they'd love some company.

Nancy hoped Joe and Frank would have time for sightseeing at some of the city's hot spots—Graceland, Beale Street, the Great American Pyramid. She had asked Ned to join her, but he was busy with final exams. Her friend George Fayne, who was Bess's cousin, couldn't leave her part-time job. So Nancy took a flight down with Bess.

The two girls unpacked and took turns in the shower. After she had dressed, Nancy surveyed herself in the room's full-length mirror. The deep blue of her blouse matched her eyes exactly, while the close-fitting white slacks accentuated her slender figure and long legs.

"You look terrific, Nan," Bess said. She was wearing a black and white loose pullover with her skirt now. With a laugh, she added, "Let's go see what kind of trouble Frank and Joe want to drag us into."

"We don't have to get involved in their case," Nancy reminded her. "We're just along for fun."

Downstairs, the girls couldn't help looking around the lobby before finding the Hardys. It was a large open space, two stories high. Tables and chairs, sofas, and large potted plants filled the center area, which was plushly carpeted. On one side of the room a man in a tuxedo played romantic tunes on a grand piano, and a bar with a mirror behind it lined the opposite wall. Overhead, a balcony ran around the edge of the room, held up by marble pillars. A wide stairway led to the second floor and the hotel's ballrooms.

In the middle of the lobby was a small marble pool with a fountain in the center. Ducks swam in it, taking no notice of the people around them. Occasionally the ducks would quack or splash some water onto the rug.

Nancy looked up at the balcony, where several men in white jackets were pushing carts of food. It looked as if they were preparing for a reception or party.

"Nancy!"

Nancy smiled as she turned in the direction of the voice and spotted Frank Hardy standing near the duck pool. Frank stood an inch over six feet, and had dark hair and brown eyes. His lean good looks were something Nancy had always found attractive, especially after not seeing him for a while.

As soon as she had the thought, Nancy shook it away. She and Frank were good friends, and that was all. Nancy would always have Ned, and Frank had his girlfriend, Callie Shaw.

"Hey! Over here." This time it was Frank's brother, Joe, who was calling and waving to Nancy. Seventeen years old, Joe was a year younger than Frank and had rugged blond good looks, blue eyes, and a broad, muscular build.

Nancy and Bess exchanged hugs with the brothers.

"You look great." Joe held Bess at arm's length and grinned. "I'll take midwestern blondes over southern belles any day."

Frank elbowed him in the ribs. "I don't know, Joe," he teased. "You were eyeing quite a few of the belles before Bess arrived."

"Don't worry," Bess said, laughing. "I know all about Joe's reputation as a flirt." She was clearly enjoying his attention.

"What's with the ducks?" Nancy asked, pointing to the pool.

"A Peabody tradition." Frank laughed. "At

eleven in the morning the ducks ride the elevator down from a tank upstairs. A guy rolls a red carpet from the elevator to the fountain. Then the ducks parade across the lobby and climb into the pool. At four o'clock they do the same in reverse."

Nancy shook her head. "Sounds kind of hokey to me."

Joe shrugged. "Hey, it beats ending up on somebody's dinner table—at least from the duck's point of view."

"It's almost four now," Bess pointed out. "We might as well stay for the show."

They sat down on a bench next to the fountain. "While we're waiting, why don't we fill you in on our case?" Frank asked.

"I thought you'd never ask." Nancy grinned.

Leaning forward and speaking in a hushed tone, Frank gave the girls some background information. "About ten years ago a high-level Network agent named Grady set up an operation in what was then East Germany."

Nancy nodded. She and Bess both knew that the Hardys sometimes worked with the Network, a supersecret intelligence agency.

"Grady was convinced there was a traitor in the Network," Joe went on.

Bess's blue eyes went wide. "You mean a double agent?"

"Right," Frank said with a short nod. "Someone who pretended to work for the United States but who was actually spying on us, giving away classified information to East Germany. The double agent reported to a German superspy named Klaus."

"Why do all these guys have only one name?" Bess asked.

"Shh," Joe cautioned, and then looked around the lobby to see that no one was listening.

Frank continued. "Grady sent his own agent, code-named the Swallow, into East Germany to find out who the traitor was. He never revealed the Swallow's identity to anyone, not even to the Network. If the double agent found out who the Swallow was, he'd tell Klaus—and get the Swallow killed. Grady claimed the Swallow was gathering lots of information, enough to put the traitor—and Klaus—out of business."

"Wow!" Nancy exclaimed. "What happened?"

Frank lowered his voice further. "A few years ago things went wrong. Grady was murdered. And since he was the Swallow's only connection, the Network lost contact with the Swallow. They couldn't even get him out of East Germany. The Swallow was trapped. For all anyone knew, he might have been killed."

"Network agents looked into Grady's double-agent theory," Joe added, "but they never figured out who it was—or if there really was one at all."

"All of this is a long way from Memphis, Tennessee," Nancy said, frowning.

"It came closer last week," Frank said. "A guy

named Hank Pritchitt called the Network. He's the house detective for the Peabody Hotel, and he claimed the Swallow was coming home. Since the Berlin Wall came down, traveling out of Germany has become easier. Apparently, the Swallow will meet with someone here in Memphis. Pritchitt has the details. He wants to sell the name of the Swallow's contact, and the Network wants to buy it."

Joe patted the briefcase he was holding. "For a *lot* of money," he added.

"I don't get it. Wouldn't the Swallow contact the Network anyway?" Nancy asked.

Frank shook his head. "The Swallow was a free-lance agent. He didn't work directly with the Network. Grady was his only contact. With Grady gone, he may not know who to trust. But the Network wants the Swallow's information badly, even if he wants to hide from them."

"They're chasing their own spy?" Bess asked, incredulous.

"Well, they want to talk to him," Joe said, "but they don't know who he is or where to find him, so they need the name of the Swallow's contact here in Memphis."

"That's where you two come in," Nancy guessed. "You're getting the info."

Frank shrugged. "No big deal. We're just passing the cash to Pritchitt after he gives us the name of the contact."

"Network errand-boy stuff," Joe mumbled.

Nancy nodded sympathetically. Although the Hardys had often done top-notch work for the Network, the agency was reluctant to trust them completely. Nancy knew from her own experience how frustrating it was not to be taken seriously as a detective simply because of her age.

"Hey! It's starting." Bess got to her feet.

Looking up, Nancy saw that a crowd had gathered around an old man in a fancy red and white uniform who stood at attention next to the marble fountain. He held a short riding crop. At his orders a big, husky boy about Nancy's age rolled out a red carpet from the elevator to the fountain. He, too, wore a red jacket and white pants, but his unruly, sandy blond hair fell over his eyes, which were bright green and lively.

Next the boy set up a portable staircase from the fountain to the carpet. He stepped aside when the old man blew a shrill note on a whistle. With his riding crop the man gently prodded the ducks toward the stairs. Protesting with indignant quacks, they climbed down the steps and waddled their way along the carpet.

As the ducks entered the elevator, the crowd burst into applause. The old man beamed, but his assistant looked slightly embarrassed.

Nancy turned as a bellhop appeared next to their sofa and said, "Excuse me, is there a Frank or Joe Hardy here?"

"I'm Frank."

"There's a message for you." The bellhop handed over a slip of paper.

Frank looked troubled as he read. "It's from Pritchitt. He says we should meet him right away at a place called Left-Hand Louie's."

"That doesn't sound good," Nancy said with a frown. Last-minute changes in plans were usually a bad sign in the world of espionage. "Wasn't the meeting supposed to be here?"

"That was the plan," Frank said.

"Where's Left-Hand Louie's?" Joe wondered.

"And *what* is it?" Bess added.

Suddenly a deep voice spoke up behind them. "I know where Louie's is."

Turning, Nancy recognized the husky teenager who'd rolled out the red carpet for the ducks. "I'm Beau Davis," he drawled with an easy grin. Nancy noticed that his eyes lingered on Bess.

"Nice to meet you." Bess held out her hand, and Beau shook it vigorously. She introduced herself, the Hardys, and Nancy.

Beau's eyes were even greener up close, Nancy noticed. And he was turning them on Bess full force. Though she blushed a little, Bess didn't show any sign of flirting with him.

"You know where Louie's is?" Frank asked.

"Sure do," Beau told him. "It's sort of a burger joint, with live music, across town."

"Near Graceland?" Bess asked hopefully. She'd talked about visiting Elvis Presley's famous home since they'd started planning the trip.

"No." Beau laughed. "Louie's is near Sun Studios, though. That's where Elvis recorded his first records. First and greatest," he added, with a tone of reverence.

"How do we get to Louie's?" Joe was eager to get to the business at hand.

"I've just finished my shift. I can take you," Beau offered. "Do you have a car?"

"No," Frank told him. "We'll take a taxi. Just tell us where it is."

"And pass up the pleasure of spending time with such lovely company?" Beau smiled at Bess.

Frank didn't like the idea of bringing a stranger along to the meet, but he didn't want to lose valuable time. "Okay," he said to Beau. "Let's go."

As they headed for the hotel entrance, Nancy heard a clattering sound overhead. She looked up at the balcony above.

Teetering precariously on the railing was a metal room-service tray. Ice cubes began to shower down, and then an ice bucket. Even as Nancy opened her mouth to call a warning, the whole tray fell over, heading straight for Frank!

Chapter

Two

"FRANK, LOOK OUT!" Nancy cried.

Frank heard the panicked sound in Nancy's voice. Instinctively he dropped to a crouch. But before he could move, he felt someone catch him around the waist and fling him backward. The two of them tumbled to the floor, and Frank's hip thudded painfully against the hard tiles.

The next thing he knew, there was a huge crash next to him, and porcelain, glass, and metal were flying everywhere. When he felt a splash of hot coffee on his arm, Frank realized it was a room service tray. Plates and glasses shattered, and a coffee urn landed with a loud explosion. Floor tiles had cracked from the impact, right where he'd been standing just a moment before.

He tried to move, but Nancy's arms were still around him. "Whoa, Nan," Frank said, managing a smile. "I'm spoken for, remember?"

With a shaky voice, Nancy said, "If I hadn't grabbed you, there wouldn't have been anything left to speak *for,* Frank Hardy."

"You guys all right?" Joe helped Frank and Nancy untangle themselves and get to their feet. A small crowd was gathering, and two bellhops appeared, looking frantic. One offered Frank a napkin to wipe the coffee off his arm. Once Frank assured them that he and Nancy were all right, the bellhops started cleaning up the wreckage.

"Talk about close calls!" Bess cried. "You could have been really hurt!"

"Joe." Nancy shot a worried glance toward the mezzanine. "Did you see anyone?"

Before she finished the question, Joe had already set the briefcase down next to his brother and was halfway up the stairs that led to the mezzanine.

A few minutes later he returned. "Nothing," he reported. "There's a cocktail party going on in one of the ballrooms, but I didn't see anyone who looked suspicious."

Bess looked startled. "Do you think someone pushed the tray down on purpose?"

"I don't know," Joe told her. "But I've learned

it's safer not to assume anything's a freak accident."

Shooting his brother a look of caution, Frank said in a strained voice, "It probably *was* just an accident, though." When Joe gave him a puzzled look, Frank motioned toward Beau.

Joe nodded his understanding and said, "Yeah, I'm sure you're right." Beau didn't know he and Frank were on a case, and it was better to keep it that way.

The hotel manager hurried over, apologizing profusely for the accident. Joe assured him they were all okay, then made an excuse about being late for an appointment. With a quick goodbye the gang hurried outside and flagged down a taxi.

"Left-Hand Louie's," Beau instructed the driver. "It's south on Union."

Nancy looked out the window as they pulled away from the curb. The Peabody Hotel was in the heart of downtown Memphis. Tall buildings of ten and fifteen stories rose on either side of the hotel. Union Avenue, a four-lane boulevard, sloped down toward the Mississippi River. On the far side of the river was Arkansas, and Nancy could see farmland there stretching for miles, with no buildings in sight.

Turning her mind back to the case, Nancy looked over at Beau and said, "Tell us about Louie's."

"Great place," said Beau, his face lighting up.

A lock of unruly hair fell in his eyes, and he pushed it aside. "I'm surprised you haven't heard about it. It's a big tourist attraction."

"Why's that?" Joe asked. He and Frank were in the front seat with the driver.

"The story goes that one day Elvis Presley dropped by Louie's place," Beau explained. "Louie liked to have musicians stop in, so he kept his own guitar in the place for them to play. Elvis picked up Louie's guitar and began strumming some chords, but suddenly he stopped.

"'Hey, Louie,' Elvis said. 'This is a doggone left-handed model.' And he handed that guitar over to Louie and said, 'You play, Left-Hand. I'll just do the singing.'"

Beau broke into a laugh, obviously delighted with the story. "And that's how Louie changed the name of his place to Left-Hand Louie's. He keeps the guitar hanging on the wall. Still lets other musicians play it, even me, now and then. Once in a while he takes it down himself and sits in with a band. It's a Memphis tradition."

"You know a lot about Memphis," Nancy commented. "Have you lived here all your life?"

Beau shrugged. "I'm new in town, but I know as much about Memphis music as anyone can."

A blues band was playing at Left-Hand Louie's when they got there. Louie's guitar hung over the bandstand, Nancy noticed, next to a portrait of Elvis. It was an electric guitar with a blue body.

The place was packed, and the band was loud. Three guitarists stood in front of the stage, the middle one singing, and behind them were the drummer and a keyboard player.

Nancy looked over the crowd, wondering if one of the people there was Pritchitt. At a large table sat a family of four—mother, father, and two young children. From the number of posters and bags piled by the table, Nancy guessed they were tourists. At another table sat a group of college students wearing T-shirts with their school's name on them. It was definitely a diverse crowd, Nancy observed.

As she followed the others to a table in the middle of the floor, she saw a lone red-haired woman at a table nearby. Nancy noticed she didn't seem to be enjoying the band.

In front of Nancy, Beau hurried to pull a chair out for Bess. Her cheeks turned pink with embarrassment as she sat down. Nancy couldn't help laughing to herself. This was a new kind of problem for Bess: trying *not* to flirt with a boy.

Soon after they sat down, a tanned girl of about eighteen approached the table. She was wearing faded jeans and a denim work shirt buttoned down the front and tied in a knot at her waist. Her lustrous brown hair was pulled back in a ponytail, but a few strands had come loose on either side of her heart-shaped face.

"Welcome to Louie's," the girl said in a lilting voice. "Can I help you?"

Joe rushed to answer first. "You sure can. You can start by telling us your name."

Frank rolled his eyes at Nancy, and she grinned back. "Joe is at it again," she whispered.

"Jennifer," the girl told Joe. "Jennifer Pardee. I'm Louie's daughter," she added, giving Joe a warning look.

Undaunted, Joe smiled at her. "My name is Joe Hardy," he said.

Jennifer hesitated a moment before asking, "Are you from out of town?"

"Yeah," Joe answered. "In for a couple of days."

"Where are you staying?"

"The Peabody."

All at once a wide smile spread over Jennifer's face. "Nice place. Well," she said, "you should let me show you around a bit. I stop working in half an hour."

Joe's eyes lit up. "Great!"

After taking their orders, Jennifer left.

Joe turned to Frank, grinning from ear to ear. "Girls—I just can't fight them off," he said. "We've been here less than a day, and already I have a date tonight."

"I don't want to ruin your evening, but let's not forget why we came here in the first place," Frank said. Then he turned to watch the band.

Nancy let her eyes continue to wander as she listened to the music. To her right sat a man in his forties who was dressed in what looked like a southern gentleman's outfit. He wore a white suit and a white panama hat and held an elegant mahogany cane with a brass tip. He was sitting alone at a table, drinking a soda but not eating anything.

Noticing that Nancy was looking at him, the man leaned toward her. "Louie's is finished," he said. "Washed up."

"Excuse me?" Nancy said.

"Look around you." The man motioned with his cane. "You can revel in old glory only so long." He paused, then seemed to remember something. "I'm sorry," he told her. "Let me introduce myself. I'm Jefferson Eliot. Just call me Jeff." He tapped his chest. "I represent the future."

Nancy raised an eyebrow. "What future?"

"The future of Memphis. The future of entertainment." He leaned forward. "The Great American Pyramid."

"Oh," Nancy said, nodding politely. She'd heard about the complex, which was built in the shape of a huge pyramid. "I haven't been there yet."

"I've opened a restaurant there. The Rock Spot. Leaves this dump in the dust. You should really come see it."

Nancy nodded again.

All of a sudden shouts broke out from across the room. Nancy and Jeff turned. A young waiter backed out of the kitchen, followed by a large man with slicked-down, graying hair who continued to yell. He wore loose jeans and a white T-shirt. Gesturing wildly, he shouted, "That's the last dish you're going to break! I'm sick of this. You're fired!"

"You see," Jeff whispered, leaning forward. "Mismanagement. This sort of outburst shouldn't happen in a restaurant. It's undignified." He let out a sigh, then stood up. Tipping his hat to her, he turned and walked toward the newly unemployed waiter.

"What was that all about?" Bess asked.

Nancy turned back to her friends. "The man seems to be the owner of a rival restaurant. Not such a nice guy, if you ask me. He was putting Louie's down."

"Well, I like this place." Bess grinned, nodding toward the band. "This music is great. I never realized I liked blues before."

"Blues is the finest kind of music there is, in my opinion," Beau said, drumming on the table and bobbing his head to the beat. He looked to the Hardys to back him up. Joe smiled back, but Frank seemed preoccupied and was looking anxiously around.

"Let me show you." Beau got up and walked to the bandstand, where the musicians were just concluding a number. "Louie!" he shouted, looking at the large man who'd just yelled at the waiter. "Let me sit in. Can I play your guitar?"

"Sure, Beau," Louie called from across the room. "You play it nice and sweet."

Beau took the guitar off the wall. One of the musicians handed him a patch cord, and he plugged it into an amplifier. For a moment the band huddled around him as he told them what to play. Then the bluesy chords filled the restaurant.

"Wow!" Joe exclaimed, impressed.

Beau's eyes were shut tight. He squeezed the neck of the guitar, coaxing out crying melodies. The audience shouted encouragement and clapped wildly. Everyone loved it.

Beau finished to loud applause. He bowed shyly, then held the guitar in the air and shouted to Louie, "This is the greatest guitar in the world! Let me buy it from you, Louie."

"Not a chance!" Louie shouted back good-naturedly. "Without that guitar Left-Hand Louie's would be nothing."

Beau hung the guitar back on the wall, then walked back to the table, his green eyes shining.

As Beau sat down, Joe slapped him on the back. "That was dynamite!"

Frank's expression lightened for a moment as he gave Beau a warm smile. "Yeah, really great," he said distractedly. Then he frowned and turned to his brother. "I'm getting worried."

"Yeah," Joe said, his blue eyes darting over the restaurant. "Pritchitt still hasn't shown."

"Pritchitt?" Beau asked.

A tense silence came over the table as the four friends realized they had slipped.

"Yeah," was all Frank said, but Nancy noticed the uneasy edge in his voice.

"Hank Pritchitt?" Beau emphasized loudly.

Joe nodded. "That's right."

Beau scowled. "What do you want with that creep?"

"Huh?" Frank looked shocked.

Nancy leaned forward. "What do you know about him?" she asked.

Beau clenched his fist on the table. "Just that he's a swindler. He works at the Peabody with me. At least, he's supposed to work. He's the house detective, but he spends most of the time playing poker in the staff lounge with a bunch of his buddies."

Frowning, Beau continued. "I came to Memphis looking to make a record at Sun Studios. Pritchitt said he could help me land a deal, but he wanted a little cash to help influence some people. I gave him just about everything I had. Then he suddenly claimed I never gave him anything. Says it's my word against his, and who's going to believe a guitar picker from out of town?"

"That's terrible!" Bess cried.

"Don't I know it," Beau said. "When I think of the right way to do it, I'm going to—"

Beau's statement was cut short by the sound of a loud bang from outside the restaurant. A silence seized the room. Everyone froze, and Nancy felt a sick sensation in the pit of her stomach. Looking at the Hardys, she saw them exchange a knowing look.

"That was a gunshot," Frank said grimly, looking at Joe.

"Pritchitt," Joe replied, guessing what was in his brother's mind.

Joe was barely out of his chair when a second shot rang out.

Chapter

Three

J OE BURST THROUGH the door and onto the sidewalk in front of Louie's restaurant. He swiveled his head quickly left, then right, but saw no one.

"Joe, look out!" he heard Nancy yell from the doorway.

From behind Louie's a beat-up red pickup truck careened wildly out of the parking lot and then over a curb, screeching across the sidewalk as it turned. Joe leapt back, narrowly avoiding being hit. The truck lurched and bounced onto the street, barely missing a passing station wagon.

Joe tried to get a glimpse of the driver, but with

the truck shaking up and down, it was impossible to see him clearly. He did notice that another person sat next to the driver but couldn't make out any features.

"Here comes another one!" Frank yelled as a second vehicle whipped around the side of Louie's. This one was a sleek black sedan. It shot across the sidewalk and into the street, and several loudly honking cars had to swerve to avoid it.

This time Joe was able to catch a glimpse of the driver through the car's open window. Two things stood out about him. He had a blond crew cut and a scar over his lip.

Joe darted into the street and started running after the two vehicles, but the horn of a passing bus brought him to his senses. He hopped back onto the sidewalk, breathing heavily.

"Do you think one of those guys was Pritchitt?" asked Nancy as she and Frank approached Joe.

"I don't know," Joe said grimly, still looking down the street. "But whoever it was, I don't like it."

"What happened?" Bess asked in a high voice. "Did you see anything?"

Turning around, Joe saw that Bess and Beau were at the front of a crowd of people that had spilled out of Louie's. Oh, great, thought Joe. Just what we need—a bunch of strangers getting in the way of our case.

As if reading his mind, Frank walked over and began waving people back into the restaurant. "It's all over. There's nothing more to see."

Louie came out of the restaurant and put his hand on a waiter's shoulder. In a low voice the restaurant owner said, "Check around back. See that everything's all right. And call the police." Then he turned to the crowd. "Let's go back inside, folks," he announced. "Enjoy the music."

Beau tapped Bess's shoulder eagerly. "See that?" he asked, pointing across the street.

Bess looked nervously in the direction he indicated. "What? Is it someone with a gun?"

"No, no," he said, grinning at her. "That's Sun Studios. Someday I'm going to record there. You just watch me."

Bess let out a nervous laugh. "Oh, that's great. I mean, I hope it happens."

Jeff Eliot pushed forward. Placing a hand on Beau's arm, he said, "You're quite a musician, son."

"Thanks," Beau said.

"You'll have to play at the Rock Spot some time."

Beau broke into a grin. "That'd be great," he said. "Where's the Rock Spot?"

Jeff looked annoyed. "The Pyramid, son. The Great American Pyramid. Give me your number so I can call you about it." He walked off toward the restaurant, tapping the brass tip of his cane on the sidewalk.

"Hey, Frank," Joe said, glancing at the waiter Louie had sent to check the parking lot. "I'm going to ask that guy some questions. I'll meet you inside, okay?"

When Joe rejoined them at their table a few minutes later, Nancy saw that he was frowning. "I talked to the guy and then walked around the parking lot myself," he told the others. "There was nothing there that looked suspicious."

Joe's face lit up in a big smile a moment later when Jennifer Pardee pulled up a chair and sat next to him.

"Mind if I join you?" she asked. "My shift's over now."

Joe didn't seem to mind at all, Nancy noticed. He started asking Jennifer all about Memphis. Next to him, Beau turned in his chair to watch the band as the music started up again.

Seeing that he and Jennifer were both distracted, Nancy leaned close to Frank and asked, "Do you think there's any point in waiting for Pritchitt now?"

"There's not much else we can do," he said, shrugging. "For a little while, at least. We can't be sure he was in one of those cars."

Having overheard Frank, Joe spoke up. "The guy in the sedan definitely wasn't Pritchitt." He described the blond-haired man with the scar.

"How do you know it wasn't Pritchitt? You haven't met him, have you?" Nancy asked him.

"No," said Joe. He pulled a photograph out of his back pocket and handed it to her. "But here's what he looks like."

Nancy examined the photo. It showed a man of about forty, with narrow lips and a prominent Adam's apple. His hair was beginning to go gray, and his skin was pockmarked.

"Could this be the guy who drove the pickup truck?" she asked him.

"Maybe," Joe replied. "I didn't get a good look. All I know is there were two people in it."

From across the table, Beau asked, "You say it was a truck? Pritchitt drives a pickup—a battered old red thing." He frowned. "What's this all about, anyway?"

Nancy saw the troubled look that came into Frank's face. She wasn't sure what he was more upset about—that Beau had overheard their conversation or that the red truck might be Pritchitt's.

After an uneasy pause Frank replied, "It's nothing important—probably just a coincidence." He turned to Nancy. "We'll give it a few more minutes here, then we'll leave." From the tone of his voice Nancy gathered he didn't want to keep talking about Pritchitt with Jennifer and Beau at the table.

"So," Frank said quickly, before Beau could ask any more questions, "you like that guitar, Beau?"

Beau broke into a grin. "It's a beauty," he said.

"I love those old guitars. They get such a full tone."

"It did sound good," Nancy said.

"Yeah," said Beau, then his face took on a puzzled expression. "The only thing is, it had a funny rattle. You probably couldn't hear it through the amplifier, but it bugged me a little."

"A rattle?" Joe echoed.

Beau nodded. "Probably a loose wire inside or something. Easy to fix." He turned to Jennifer. "You think you could talk your dad into selling it to me?"

"Not a chance," Jennifer said, shaking her head adamantly. "That guitar keeps people coming here—at least, that's the way my dad sees it."

As if struck by a sudden idea, the pretty brunette turned to Joe. "Come and meet my dad, Joe. If he likes you, maybe I can show you around Memphis a bit."

Joe laughed, slightly embarrassed, but he followed Jennifer into the kitchen.

He came back a moment later, smiling. Apparently, he'd passed inspection.

"I guess I just bowled him over with my natural charm," he cracked, ignoring the loud groans from Frank, Nancy, and Bess. "But seriously, there's no point in staying here any longer. Let's see some of this town's nightlife."

"All right!" said Bess. "Look out, Memphis, here we come."

* * *

"How do I look?" asked Bess, turning so Nancy got the full effect of her black dress, tights, and boots.

They had all gone back to the hotel to change before going out. Jennifer was waiting in the lobby.

"Terrific," said Nancy. "I bet a certain guy won't be able to keep his green eyes off you," she teased.

"You mean Beau?" Bess asked. "Oh, he's nice—as a friend, I mean." That was all she said, but Nancy noticed she was blushing.

"We'd better go," Nancy said, checking her watch. "The others are waiting for us."

The Hardys were standing together in the lobby, conversing quietly, when Nancy and Bess got out of the elevator.

"We don't want to call attention to the brief-case," Joe said. "Leaving it in the room is the smartest way—hiding it in plain sight. Besides, Pritchitt probably has a key to the hotel's safe, so the money wouldn't be any better off there."

"I just hope it doesn't get *stolen* in plain sight," Frank said.

"Where's your date, Romeo?" Bess asked, punching Joe lightly on the arm. "I don't see Jennifer."

Joe pointed across the lobby. "Over there. She had to make a phone call."

"And here comes Beau," Nancy said.

"You look great, Bess!" he exclaimed as he approached the group. Then, looking embarrassed, he told her, "I'm sorry, but I can't join you."

"What?" Bess looked surprised—and a little disappointed.

"I only remembered when I got back. There's something I have to do tonight. I hope you have fun, though." Beau made a motion as if he were tipping his hat, though he wasn't wearing one. Then he sauntered through the lobby doors.

Jennifer came hurrying across the lobby. "You all ready for some fun?" she asked.

"Definitely," Joe answered.

At Jennifer's instructions they took a cab to a place called Overton Square. It was located in midtown Memphis, away from the tall buildings that surrounded the Peabody and the rest of downtown. There were several cafés and nightspots in the square, and the warm Memphis night had brought out a cheerful crowd.

Jennifer was full of information and funny stories about the town. Frank could see what his brother liked about her. Being Louie's daughter, she seemed to know plenty of people. And Joe certainly wasn't losing any time getting to know her. Frank saw Joe casually slip his arm through Jennifer's.

"I could get to like it here," Joe said.

"Well, that's nice," she said. Suddenly she let

Joe's arm drop to wave to an acquaintance who passed by, and Frank thought she seemed nervous. Maybe Joe was pushing things too quickly.

Jennifer led them to an outdoor café, and they all sat down and ordered dinner. Joe and Jennifer launched into a private conversation, while Bess asked the waiter about several items on the menu.

Leaning back in his chair, Frank said, "This is the life, huh, Nancy?"

Nancy smiled. "That's for sure." She sighed. "But I wish Ned were here."

Frank nodded. He seemed a bit wistful as well. "I wish Callie were around, too."

For a moment they both stared off into space. Then they looked back at each other and broke into laughter. "Listen to us whine," Nancy said.

After dinner the group strolled in the park, where performers were entertaining small groups of onlookers. At a little past midnight they took a taxi back to the hotel, dropping Jennifer off at home on the way. The girls' hotel room was on the same floor as the Hardys, and they rode the elevator up together.

"Well," said Frank as they got off at the third floor and began walking down the hall. "I think we've done everything we can for today. Until Pritchitt contacts us, all we can do is assume that either he's changed his mind or something's happened to him."

Joe raked a hand through his blond hair. "I say we rent a car and comb the town looking for that red pickup truck."

"Can't you just call the police?" asked Bess.

"No one's done anything wrong that we know of," Nancy reminded her.

"Besides," said Frank, pushing open the door to his and Joe's room, "the Network wouldn't appreciate it." He flicked on the light.

"Frank!" Nancy gasped.

The room was a mess. Drawers were pulled open, and clothes lay strewn everywhere. Two suitcases had been overturned on the beds. Joe ran to the closet, threw open the door, and dug frantically in the pile of clothes on the floor.

"The money!" he shouted, turning a horrified look toward the others. "It's gone!"

Chapter

Four

"I DON'T BELIEVE THIS," Frank moaned, sitting down on one of the beds. "We blew our mission. The Network is going to kill us."

Nancy and Bess walked into the room and sat on the other bed. "Don't you think you'd better call the front desk?" Nancy suggested.

Frank made the call, and five minutes later Tad Baker arrived.

"This is really terrible," Baker told them, surveying the room in dismay as Frank and Joe explained what had happened. "Let me assure you this is not a common occurrence here at the Peabody. And to top it off, our house detective is missing."

"Hank Pritchitt?" Nancy asked.

Tad looked puzzled. "Yeah," he said. "How did you know?"

"I've just heard his name around," Nancy said quickly. Frank and Joe didn't want Tad to know what their mission was, or how they knew Pritchitt.

"What do you mean, he's missing?" Nancy asked, worried.

"We haven't seen him for two days," Tad said.

"Not at all?" Frank pressed. "Not even passing through?"

"No," said Tad. "If I *did* see him, I'd be telling him to report to the manager—pronto."

"Hmm." Frank frowned, thinking hard. Between the gunshots at Louie's, their money being stolen, and Pritchitt's disappearance, things weren't looking good.

Frank turned to Tad. "You should get the police in here. Have them dust for prints and anything else they need to do. We'll be waiting in the coffee shop in the lobby."

"Check," said Tad. He reached for the phone.

Nancy, Bess, and the Hardys went down to the coffee shop and took a table in an empty corner. There was only one waitress on duty at that late hour.

"The way I see it," Nancy said after the waitress had brought them four sodas, "whoever broke into your room knew you had that money."

She frowned. "As Tad said, break-ins aren't all that common at the Peabody. A burglar usually tries to find out who's staying in what room before making a hit. There's not much sense in breaking into a room where there's nothing of value to steal. And let's face it. You're a couple of teenagers—hardly hot prospects for a burglar."

"Nancy's right," said Frank. "I don't think we were the victims of a random robbery."

Bess spoke up. "Didn't this Pritchitt guy know you'd have money?"

"Sure," said Joe.

"And isn't he the house detective here?" Bess said, growing excited. "He'd even have a passkey, wouldn't he?"

Nancy frowned. "Yes, but I don't think it was Pritchitt," she said, taking a sip of her soda. "He was going to get that money anyway. Why would he have to steal it?"

"Maybe he really didn't have any information," Joe suggested. "Or maybe he was nervous we'd double-cross him, so he double-crossed us first."

Frank shook his head. "I think he had some valuable information," he said. "The Network seemed pretty certain that he was for real. Double-crossing is a possibility."

"Maybe you should call the Network," Nancy suggested. "Tell them what's happened."

Frank winced at the idea. Nancy saw he wasn't

eager to tell the Network about the stolen money. "I'll wait till morning," he said.

"Sorry we're late," Frank said as he and Joe joined Bess and Nancy in the hotel coffee shop for breakfast the following morning. "I just got off the phone with the Gray Man."

"The Gray Man?" Bess repeated. "Who's that?"

"He's our contact with the Network," Joe explained, sitting down and taking a look at one of the menus. "He gave us this assignment."

"And now he *regrets* giving us this assignment," Frank amended, grimacing. "He wasn't pleased to find out that Pritchitt stood us up last night. Finding the Swallow's contact is a high priority for the Network. When I told him about the stolen money, the Gray Man gave me the usual grief about our age, saying he should never have trusted us."

Nancy gave Frank a sympathetic look. "This sounds serious."

Just then a waitress came to take their order. Frank waited until they were alone again, then said, "Well, the stakes are getting higher. Remember I told you about that German superspy—Klaus?"

"The one the Swallow was secretly collecting information about?" Bess asked.

Frank nodded. "That's the one. Well, nobody

at the Network is sure who Klaus really is. They do know about one of his henchmen, though. Klaus has a couple of top agents he takes with him on important cases. One of these guys was spotted coming through customs last week. He was flying under an assumed name. When the Gray Man checked the ticketing information on this guy, it turned out that his final destination was Memphis."

"If one of Klaus's top agents is here, then Klaus is probably in Memphis, too," Nancy guessed. "And they wouldn't have come unless they knew that the Swallow was coming home."

Joe nodded. "You can bet that he's not here to visit Elvis's mansion."

"The Gray Man warned us about Klaus," Frank said soberly. "He's ruthless and deadly, and the Swallow is a big threat to him. Klaus will do almost anything to keep the Swallow from delivering information about him to the Network."

The waitress brought their orders, and they started in on their plates of pancakes. A pensive mood hung over the table as they ate.

Then Bess spoke up. "And I thought this would be a vacation. Relaxing, seeing the sights . . ." She tried to laugh, but Nancy saw the fear in her blue eyes.

"Hey, Bess," said Joe, placing his hand on her arm. "There's no reason for you and Nancy to get involved in this. After all, it's our case. You guys should just have fun, do whatever you want."

"No." Bess shook her head determinedly. "I'm going to help." She looked at Nancy. "Friends need to stick together."

Nancy grinned at the Hardys. "And I'm *always* up for a new case. So, what should we do?"

"Thanks, guys," Frank said. His voice became brisk as he continued. "There are two things. One, we need to go to Pritchitt's house. And second, there are Pritchitt's poker buddies— Beau mentioned them last night. Maybe one of them knows something about what Pritchitt was up to or why he disappeared."

"We should split up," Joe said. "Frank, you and Nancy can go out to Pritchitt's place. Bess and I will track down Pritchitt's buddies."

"You mean we should pretend we're a couple?" said Bess, batting her eyes at Joe and grabbing his arm.

Nancy laughed. "I don't think you need to lay it on that thick. Besides," she added, giving Joe a teasing wink, "after last night I think Joe's preoccupied with another girl."

After breakfast Joe and Bess went off to find Beau and ask about the poker player Pritchitt knew. Meanwhile, Frank and Nancy found a phone book next to the bank of telephones in the lobby. After looking up Pritchitt's address, they headed for the hotel cab stand.

They gave the driver Pritchitt's address, and Nancy traced their progress on a map as the taxi drove down to Front Street, then turned north. To the left lay the Mississippi River. On the shore, just off Front Street, was a large marina.

"Hey, look at that," Frank said. "Old-fashioned riverboats." Near where they were docked, a sign advertised cruises up the river.

"What's that?" Nancy asked, pointing. Next to the riverboat dock a street plunged straight into the water. Next to this ramp sat a collection of odd vehicles. They looked like boats, but they had wheels.

"Those are Delta Ducks," said the cab driver. "Amphibious vehicles. They drive through town, then up the river. Tourists love 'em."

The driver was apparently used to pointing out landmarks. "Over there is Mud Island," he went on, flicking his thumb toward the river. A few hundred yards offshore Nancy saw the long, narrow island he was referring to. "There's a river museum on it—a replica of the whole Mississippi River, from its start, up near Minneapolis, to where it empties into the Gulf of Mexico. You get to it by this tramway."

The cab was passing by the entrance to the tram. Nancy saw a stairway leading to an elevated walkway that stretched over the water. Underneath, a cable car dangled from its track.

"That looks like fun," Nancy commented to

Frank. "We'll have to go there when we've wrapped up the case."

"And now," said the driver, becoming theatrical, "we come to the Great American Pyramid!"

Nancy had to admit that the Pyramid was impressive. Sitting at the edge of the river, it was three hundred feet high and covered with stainless steel that shone like silver in the sunlight. An elevator ran diagonally up two corners on the outside of the Pyramid.

"Inside is a sports arena, a music museum, a restaurant . . ." The driver ticked each place off on his fingers as he spoke.

"And the Rock Spot," Nancy added, recalling her conversation with Jeff Eliot.

"Yeah," said the driver.

Beyond the Pyramid the city thinned out. Tall buildings gave way to smaller houses and wide stretches of land. The taxi continued north for about ten more minutes, then pulled to a stop in front of a small, beat-up shack.

"Here you are," the driver announced.

Nancy and Frank got out. Noticing that there were just a few houses and no stores or public phones in sight, Frank gave the driver some money and said, "Could you meet us back here in an hour?"

"Sure thing," the cab driver said. With a quick wave, he drove off.

Pritchitt's house was only one story high. Its

green paint was peeling, and the lawn needed mowing. His truck wasn't in the driveway. Frank knocked on the door, but there was no response. When he tried to open it, he found it was locked.

"Let's check the windows," Nancy suggested.

In the back they found an unlocked window. At first it didn't budge when Frank pushed on it. But after a moment he felt it give way, lurching up with a resistant screech. Frank looked quickly around to make sure no one was in sight. Then he climbed through the window.

Nancy was standing next to him in the kitchen a moment later. There wasn't much in the room—a table with a few items on it, a refrigerator, a stove, counters, and one cabinet. Dirty dishes were piled in the sink.

"I'll check out the rest of the house." Frank disappeared through the room's only doorway.

Going over to the table, Nancy saw an envelope full of photographs, a pad of paper, and a pencil. An empty glass sat nearby.

She picked up the photographs and began flipping through them. They seemed to be of Pritchitt's poker buddies—four men sitting around a card table. They made faces in some of the pictures, tried to look serious in others. Pritchitt himself wasn't in any of the shots. He must have been behind the camera, Nancy assumed. One of the other men was Louie, the restaurant owner. Another man looked familiar, but Nancy couldn't place him.

On impulse she counted the photos. Thirty-five. That's strange, she thought. Usually a roll of film has thirty-six pictures.

Her curiosity aroused, she fished in the envelope for the negatives. There were thirty-six exposures on the negatives.

So why was the picture missing?

Suddenly Nancy had an idea. Picking up the pad of paper that had been sitting next to the photos, she moved it so that it caught the light from the window at different angles. There were faint impressions from where a pencil had drawn on an upper sheet.

Growing excited, Nancy took a pencil and ran it lightly over the surface of the page. Where the paper was indented, white lines formed words against the pencil-gray background.

"Frank!" Nancy yelled. "I've found something —something important!"

Chapter

Five

FRANK WAS BACK in the kitchen in about two seconds flat. "What is it?"

Nancy showed him the pad of paper. The words *Gulf of Mexico—Thursday, midnight* were spelled in white letters where she had run the pencil across the indentations.

"Sounds like a meeting place," she said.

Frank stared at her for a second. "But not a very specific location." He raked a hand through his wavy brown hair. "It does seem like a meeting place, though. But, Nancy, the Gulf of Mexico spans hundreds of miles. We have to have something better than that to go on."

Nancy nodded, frowning. "Maybe that's all

Pritchitt knew. Look, Frank—here's something else." Nancy pointed to a faint white circle that had appeared above the writing.

Frank frowned. "What do you make of it?"

"Check this out. There are thirty-five pictures here." She held up the photos. "But there are thirty-six exposures on the negatives."

Frank's eyes lit with understanding. "Maybe the missing photo shows the Swallow's contact."

Nancy nodded excitedly. "I bet the circle came from Pritchitt marking the photo to show who the contact is. Sure, it's a long shot," she went on in a rush. "But it does make sense." Nancy showed him the negatives. "All thirty-six pictures are of the same four guys. He must have circled the contact on the photo that's missing. I think that note and the picture are what Pritchitt was going to give you and Joe at Left-Hand Louie's last night."

Frank let out a low whistle. "What went wrong? More to the point, what can we do about this now that Pritchitt's disappeared?" He tucked the negatives into his shirt pocket. "Even if we use these to get a copy of the missing shot, we won't know which of the men Pritchitt circled."

"Right," said Nancy. "We'll have to check out all the men. Let's take one of the other shots so we'll have an idea of who the suspects are. Maybe Joe and Bess will be able to identify the men after they've talked to Beau."

"Good idea." Frank sorted through the photos, picked one, and slipped it into his pocket.

They looked around for another ten minutes but found nothing. After climbing back out the kitchen window, they walked around the house to the driveway and waited for the taxi driver.

Frank and Nancy got back to the hotel just as Joe and Bess were leaving.

"We just finished talking to Beau," said Joe as the four teens met in the lobby.

"And?" Frank prompted.

"He gave us four names," said Joe.

"Let me guess," said Nancy. "One of them is Louie Pardee."

Joe shot her a quizzical glance. "How did you know?"

"Didn't you know she's psychic?" Frank said with a wink for Nancy. Then, becoming serious, he explained about the note, the photograph, and the Gulf of Mexico. "There's a strong possibility that the Swallow's contact is one of Pritchitt's poker buddies," he concluded.

"Makes sense," said Joe. "Pritchitt is probably close to those four guys. He would have had a good chance of finding out about the Swallow through one of them."

Joe pulled a small notepad from his back pocket. "Here are the rest of the names, besides Louie. First there's Ernest Teague. He's the curator and tour guide of the *Memphis Belle*. That's a

World War Two bomber plane that's on display at Mud Island."

"We passed there on our way to Pritchitt's," Nancy said. "It looks like a neat place."

"Next," Joe went on, "is Bill Cooper. Captain Billy, Beau called him. He's the captain of a riverboat called the *River Queen* that carries tour cruises up the Mississippi."

Frank nodded. "We passed that, too. Who else is there?"

"Jack Arvis, Beau's boss. He's the guy who leads the ducks across the carpet."

"Of course!" Nancy exclaimed, snapping her fingers. "That was the other familiar face in the photograph."

"Well, what are we waiting for?" Joe put his pad away. "Let's start talking to some of these guys. Maybe one is planning a trip to the Gulf of Mexico on Thursday."

Frank nodded. "The riverboat landing is pretty close to the Mud Island tramway," he pointed out. "Both are in walking distance. Why don't we head on over?"

The four of them walked down to Front Street, then separated. This time they decided that Nancy and Bess would look for Bill Cooper while the Hardys checked up on Ernest Teague.

As Nancy and Bess walked toward the riverboats, Bess observed, "This is like walking back in time."

The riverboat was long and flat, with a huge

paddlewheel at its stern, each blade as big as a tabletop. Dual smokestacks, black and ornate, rose out of the boat's middle. The cabin stretched from front to back. It was decorated with fancy woodwork and had windows all around it. Nancy could see that inside was a large dining room. Apparently, the boat was used for dinner cruises.

"The *River Queen*," Nancy read aloud off the ship's hull. "This is it."

"I don't see anyone," Bess said, pausing on the dock and glancing around.

"It's not normal business hours for them," Nancy replied. "But there's got to be somebody on board. Look." She pointed to the gangplank. The chain, which normally stretched across as a barrier, was hanging loose.

Nancy started up the gangplank, with Bess following hesitantly. "Are you sure it's all right to go up there?" Bess asked.

"Sure. If Bill Cooper is on board, he's probably near there," Nancy said, pointing to a separate cabin on the second level. Finding a ladder, the girls climbed up.

Near the door of the upper cabin they saw a man crouching over a metal bin. Several life preservers lay scattered around him.

"Excuse me," said Nancy.

The man turned his head to them, surprised. He was tall and in his mid-thirties. Nancy recognized him from Pritchitt's photographs, though she thought he looked more handsome in real life. His hair was dark brown. His eyes were brown and friendly, though at the moment Nancy thought she detected some tension in them.

"Are you Captain Cooper?" Nancy asked, even though she was quite sure of the answer.

"Yes," Cooper replied, closing the lid of the storage bin and straightening up. He seemed to relax a bit. "I was just reorganizing these life preservers. Trying to keep things from getting tangled up in there."

"I'm Nancy Drew," Nancy said, "and this is Bess Marvin."

"Delighted." Cooper shook their hands. "Bill Cooper. What can I do for you? Let's step into my office. I can leave the life preservers for later." He led the girls to his cabin. Then he laid a hand on the steering wheel and turned to face them.

"I'm looking for a friend of yours," Nancy began. "Hank Pritchitt."

Cooper studied her for a moment. Then he said, "Have you tried the Peabody Hotel? That's where he works."

Nancy nodded. "He hasn't shown up there in two days."

"Hmm," said Bill Cooper. "Well, I guess that's not unlike him." He gave them an easy grin. His voice was deep and warm, and Nancy found herself smiling back.

"Have you seen him recently?" she asked.

"Nope," said Cooper. "Can't say that I have. The last time I saw him was Friday night. Our poker game." He gave them an apologetic look.

"Hmm," said Nancy. "Well, if you do see him, could you have him give me a call at the hotel?"

"Sure will," Cooper replied.

Bess had been looking out the window of the cabin. "This is a great boat," she commented. "Do you run cruises every night?"

Bill Cooper nodded proudly. "Every evening at six. Six to eight."

"We should go some night," Nancy said to Bess. Then an idea occurred to her. Giving Bess a meaningful look, Nancy added, "Maybe Thursday."

"Sure," Cooper said warmly. "Glad to have you."

"Will you be the captain on Thursday evening?" Nancy asked, recalling that that was the night of the midnight rendezvous on the Gulf of Mexico.

He nodded. "I'm the captain every night."

Well, scratch *him* off the list of suspects, Nancy thought. Aloud, she said, "Good. Maybe we'll see you then."

Cooper grinned. "It'd be my pleasure."

"Who's this?" Bess stared at a photograph tacked to the wall. "She's beautiful."

Glancing at the picture, Nancy had to agree. The photo was of a lovely woman with long black hair, brown eyes like Cooper's, and creamy skin.

"Well, she's sort of my girlfriend," Cooper said. "Name's Madeline. I haven't seen her in quite a while, but I hope to soon."

He seemed embarrassed, so Nancy changed the subject. "Well, thanks," she told him, urging Bess toward the door. "See you Thursday."

Cooper gave them a nod. "Looking forward to it," he said.

The girls made their way down to the lower deck and left the steamboat.

"Let's go see how Frank and Joe are doing," Nancy suggested.

She and Bess started walking up the pavement, but a sudden honk brought them up short. Looking up, they watched in surprise as an odd little boat on wheels drove past them. It turned onto a stretch of asphalt that led straight down into the river, similar to the one Nancy and Frank had seen from their taxi earlier. Tourists filled the deck of the funny boat, and they crowed with delight as the boat made its way across the water, disappearing around the bottom tip of Mud Island.

"That's one of the Delta Ducks," Nancy told Bess. "Hey—look!" She pointed up at the tramway.

Frank and Joe were waving from inside a cable car that was just pulling in. Nancy and Bess waved back, then walked toward the tramway entrance. No sooner did they reach it than Frank and Joe met them.

"We didn't get much," said Joe, "except that Ernest Teague is not our man."

"He broke his leg two days ago," Frank informed them. "The guy who's replacing him told us he'll be in the hospital for another week and a half. How did you do?"

"Cooper hasn't seen Pritchitt since Friday," Nancy explained as the four teens started walking back toward the hotel. "And he's going to be working on the boat Thursday night."

Frank nodded. "So he's probably not the contact, either."

"We still have to talk to Arvis," Nancy said.

During the walk back to the hotel, Joe launched into an enthusiastic description of Mud Island to them. "The best thing," he concluded, "is this model of the Mississippi River. It's a half-mile long and goes down the island. And at the bottom tip it empties into this huge pool where people can swim."

"Like the ocean," Bess said. "Neat."

"Yeah," said Joe. "Too bad we didn't bring our bathing suits."

"You know," Frank said to Joe, "we're covering a lot of ground on foot. We might as well rent a car. What do you think?"

Joe nodded. "I think I saw a place down the street."

Bess decided to join them, but Nancy said she'd wait for them in the lobby.

Inside the hotel Nancy's gaze immediately lit

on Beau. His tall frame looked uncomfortable in the uniform he wore to tend the ducks.

"Where's Bess?" he asked after saying hello.

"With Frank and Joe," Nancy answered. "They just went to rent a car."

"I was hoping I could show you all the town," said Beau in his drawling voice. "Especially since I missed my chance last night."

Nancy thought quickly. She didn't want Beau to know she and the others were working on the case. "That would be nice," she said after a pause. "But we've been out all morning, and we're pretty tired."

Suddenly, from across the lobby, they heard shouting. It was Louie Pardee, standing next to a police officer and pointing furiously at Beau.

"He's the thief!" Louie yelled, his round face red with anger. "He's the one who stole my guitar!"

Chapter

Six

WHAT'S THE PROBLEM, LOUIE?" Beau drawled. There was a look of confusion on his face.

Louie stormed toward Beau and Nancy, gesturing impatiently for the police officer to follow. Nancy noticed that people in the lobby were stopping to stare.

"I told you I wasn't going to sell it!" Louie shouted. "So you went and stole it."

The police officer put a hand on Louie's arm, trying to calm him. "Hold on," said the officer. "Don't go making accusations you can't prove."

"What proof do you want?" Louie yelled. "This guy drifted in from out of town, took a liking to my guitar, and stole it. Everybody heard him say he wanted it."

"He offered to buy it," Nancy corrected, stepping in between Louie and Beau. "That has nothing to do with stealing."

Louie glared at her.

The officer pointed a finger at Beau. "I will say this much, though. It doesn't look good that we found you lurking around Sun Studios last night. That was around the time of the robbery—and right across the street."

Concerned, Nancy turned to Beau. "Is that true?"

Beau had stood silently during Louie's accusation, looking bewildered. "Like I told the police last night," he said to Nancy, "I got a call from a talent scout. At least, I thought he was a talent scout. The guy claimed he'd heard me play at Louie's and wanted me to do a demo tape. He told me to come by Sun Studios at midnight."

"That's pretty late," Nancy said skeptically.

Beau shrugged. "He said he could use the studio for free late at night. Besides, midnight isn't so late for musicians. But when I got to Sun Studios, no one was there. Guess it was just a joke. I must have set off an alarm when I leaned against the windows or something. All of a sudden I was surrounded by police."

"We let him go," the officer explained to Louie and Nancy. "He hadn't really done anything wrong." He turned to Beau. "But this puts you near the scene of this robbery, so you'll have to answer a few questions. You're a prime suspect."

"I say you arrest him now," growled Louie, his face still red.

"We have no grounds to arrest him," the officer explained patiently.

Nancy put a reassuring hand on Beau's arm. She cast a swift glance at the crowd that had gathered around them. Suddenly her gaze stopped on a familiar face. It was the red-haired woman whom she'd seen at Louie's. What was she doing at the Peabody Hotel?

When Nancy turned her attention back to Beau, the officer was saying to him, "Now, son, you're not obliged to do this, but it would sure help your case if you'd take me up to your room. Let me see there's no guitar there."

Beau nodded eagerly. "None but my own," he said. "Let's go."

The husky teenager led the police officer and Louie to the elevators. Once they were gone, the crowd dispersed.

Nancy noticed the thin woman had entered the hotel coffee shop. On an impulse Nancy followed her. The woman had been at Louie's when Beau had offered to buy Louie's guitar. If she was willing to attest to that, it would help convince the police of Beau's innocence.

Approaching the woman's table, Nancy said, "Do you mind if I join you for a moment?"

The woman looked startled but gestured to an empty seat. "Why, no. Go ahead."

"My name is Nancy Drew."

"Tracy Brandt," the woman returned, giving Nancy a quick nod. Her red hair was boyishly short, and her features were angular yet very elegant. Nancy thought she was attractive in a sophisticated way. Her age was difficult to determine.

"I noticed you in Louie's yesterday," Nancy began.

Brandt smiled. "Yes. When that boy played so well. I saw what happened just now. You think he stole the guitar?"

"No," said Nancy. "In fact, that's what I want to talk to you about." She asked Ms. Brandt if she'd be willing to tell the police that she'd heard Beau offer to buy Louie's guitar.

"Of course I would," Ms. Brandt replied instantly. "I really don't believe he stole it, either."

Nancy didn't think it would be polite to just get up and leave, so she asked, "Are you from out of town? You don't have a southern accent."

Ms. Brandt laughed. "Yes. I'm here on business."

"Oh, really? What sort of business?" Nancy inquired.

Ms. Brandt leveled her gaze at Nancy. "I deal in audio equipment," she replied. "I'm setting up a stereo store in the Pyramid."

"That sounds interesting," Nancy commented. "It looks like a fun place. And Memphis must be a great town for someone involved in music."

"What?" said Brandt. "Oh, yes. You mean Elvis and Graceland and all that." Suddenly Brandt became quite talkative. "Yes, Elvis is one of my favorites. I love all his songs—'Hound Dog' . . . 'Jailhouse Rock' . . . 'Great Balls of Fire.' "

Nancy blinked. She was pretty sure "Great Balls of Fire" had been written by Jerry Lee Lewis, not Elvis Presley, but it would be rude to point that out. Smiling politely, she said, "So I guess you're staying here at the Peabody."

"I usually do," Brandt responded, "but I couldn't get a reservation this time. I do love it here, though, so I come often for tea and meals."

Nancy glanced at her watch. The Hardys and Bess should be returning any time with their rental car. "Well," she said to Ms. Brandt, "it's been nice talking to you, but I've got to go now."

She left the coffee shop. Tracy Brandt seemed like a nice enough woman, even if she was a bit uneven—cool one moment, warm the next.

In the lobby Beau was just saying goodbye to the police officer and Louie. Catching sight of Nancy, Beau smiled wearily and came over to her.

"Well, I'm still a suspect. But at least they didn't find Louie's guitar." Leaning closer to her,

Beau lowered his voice. "Hey, Nancy. I need your help."

"What for?" Nancy asked.

He shifted his husky frame from one foot to the other before saying, "If I've got this right, you and your friends seem to be some kind of detectives."

Nancy wasn't sure what to say. Telling him the truth might interfere with the Hardys' case. "Kind of," she hedged. "Why?"

"Well, I need you to help me clear my name," said Beau. "I didn't steal that guitar. The last thing in the world I need is trouble with the law."

"If you didn't steal it, you won't get in trouble," Nancy assured him. "I'm sure the police will find the real thief."

"The problem is, I think someone's trying to frame me," Beau went on earnestly. "I mean, with that phony call that led me out to Sun Studios and all. And the timing couldn't be worse."

He did have a point about the phone call, Nancy thought. "What do you mean, the timing couldn't be worse?" she pressed.

"I'm very busy right now. My boss is going out of town for a couple of days, so I've got to take care of the ducks on my own."

Nancy became suddenly alert. "Jack Arvis?" she asked. He was one of the possible suspects for the Swallow's contact.

"Yeah," Beau responded.

Nancy put a hand on Beau's shoulder. "Okay, I'll see what I can do." But she wasn't thinking of the guitar. Beau's words about his boss had set her mind racing.

The sound of a car horn caught Nancy's attention. Looking out the doors of the hotel, she saw a bright red convertible. Nancy laughed when she saw the three passengers waving to her, Joe and Bess from the front seat and Frank from the back. Saying goodbye to Beau, she hurried out the door.

"Guys," she said, grinning, "what an incredible car."

From the driver's seat Joe said, "The man at the rental agency called this the Jerry Lee Lewis special. Apparently, the singer used to cruise around Memphis in a red convertible."

"Except his was probably a Cadillac," added Frank with a sarcastic grin.

"Big deal," said Joe. He revved the engine. "This one's got more horsepower than anything Jerry Lee Lewis would have driven."

"Hop in," Bess called.

Nancy jumped in the backseat next to Frank.

"It's time to get some lunch," said Joe. "Where should we go?"

"How about there?" Nancy said, pointing. Several posters advertising the Rock Spot were plastered on a nearby telephone pole. "Isn't that Jeff Eliot's place at the Great American Pyramid?"

"Yes," said Joe, putting the car in gear. "Let's try it."

During the short drive to the Pyramid, Nancy told the others about Louie accusing Beau of stealing his guitar. She also told them what Beau had revealed about his boss. "Jack Arvis is going out of town for a couple of days."

"Today's Tuesday," Frank said. "That gives him plenty of time to get to the Gulf of Mexico for the meeting Thursday night. It looks as if he could be our man. We'll have to find him today."

Joe glanced at his brother and Nancy in the rearview mirror. "*After* lunch," he said. "There's no way I can check out leads on an empty stomach."

Up close the Pyramid was even more impressive than from the street. It rose twenty-seven stories high and looked to be almost two football fields long on each side. The incline elevators rose and descended on the outside of it. The Rock Spot was at the base of the Pyramid.

Inside, the club was an odd mix of modern architecture and rustic decor. The wooden tables had an aged look to them. Tinted photographs of rock stars hung on the walls.

"This looks like a copy of Left-Hand Louie's," Bess commented after looking around.

"But not as populated," Frank pointed out. "Look. Most of the tables are empty."

"Well, look who's here!" a voice boomed.

The four teenagers turned to see Jeff Eliot. He

was dressed in the same white suit and panama hat as the night before, Joe noticed. Jeff waved his brass-tipped cane at them. "Glad you could make it. Come for lunch?"

"Yes," Nancy said.

"Great, great. Spence," he called, "give them a great table."

"Remember him?" Nancy whispered to Frank as Spence came toward them. "He's the guy Louie fired last night when we were there."

Frank nodded. "Got a new job pretty fast."

Spence led them to a booth and placed four menus on the table. Frank and Nancy sat on one side, while Joe and Bess slid in across from them.

"Jeff Eliot is trying a little too hard," Joe said. He grimaced as he examined the menu. "Look, there's the Memphis Blues Burger. That's the same name Louie uses, for the same exact thing. Isn't one Louie's enough?"

"He seems phony," Nancy added, "with that southern gentleman getup he wears."

"Some people will do anything if it's good for business," said Frank.

"Well," Bess said optimistically, "despite everything else about this place, at least the food sounds good. What are you guys having?"

As they were trying to decide, a commotion arose. Louie Pardee came barging through the front door. "Jefferson Eliot!" he yelled. "Come out here, you coward!"

"What's going on?" Jeff said, coming out of the kitchen.

"You know what's going on, you swindler!" Louie shouted, shaking his fist. "You've been going all over town plastering your own posters right over mine."

Leaning forward, Nancy whispered to her friends, "This must be Louie's day for making accusations. First Beau, and now Jeff Eliot."

"I don't know what you're talking about," said Jeff indignantly.

Nancy noticed that two muscular bartenders were taking notice of the altercation. They put down their work and approached Louie from behind.

"Uh-oh, this looks like trouble," Nancy told the others, gesturing toward the bartenders. She held her breath as Louie raged on.

"You know your place is going nowhere!" Louie shouted. "So you spend your time covering up my promo posters. But it won't hurt my business. People want to see the bands that come to Louie's. They'll *never* come here."

"You're washed up," said Jeff, smirking. "Your days in this town are numbered."

"Why, you—" Red-faced, Louie launched himself at Jeff's chest and pushed him against a wall.

Suddenly the two bartenders were on Louie. One grabbed his arms from behind, and the other drew back his fist.

That was all the prompting the Hardys needed.

"Let's go!" shouted Joe, kicking back his chair. Frank was right behind him.

"Wait!" Nancy shouted.

But it was too late. Fists were already flying, and the Hardys were in the thick of it.

Chapter

Seven

NANCY COULDN'T BELIEVE what she was seeing. In no time at all a free-for-all was in progress.

She gasped as Joe dived at the bartender who was about to hit Louie. Joe's momentum sent them crashing onto a table, which slid a few feet and then collapsed under their weight. The brawler was punching blindly with all his strength. Joe did his best to block the man and managed to get in a few punches of his own.

Meanwhile, Frank had tackled the other bartender. He spun the man around to face him, then landed a solid punch on his jaw. The bartender careened back, stumbling on some chairs and falling to the floor. Frank grabbed his shirt and yanked him to his feet.

"Bess, we've got to stop them!" Nancy cried. She jumped to her feet and rushed over.

"Boys, boys!" Jeff yelled at the same time, while Louie, looking shaken, also tried to persuade the brawlers to stop.

"Frank! Joe!" Nancy cried. "Calm down."

Joe looked up just long enough to wink at her. "Aw, come on, Nancy. The fun's just starting." But Nancy noticed that he eased up on the bartender.

The man Joe had been fighting was pinned to the floor. With a final warning glare Joe let go of him and stood up.

Frank's opponent had also had enough. When Frank let go of his shirt, the bartender leaned against a table for support, gasping for breath.

"My, my, my," said Jeff. "What a terrible misunderstanding."

Joe could tell that his words weren't genuine. "Hey—" Joe shook a fist at Jeff. "Your stooges attacked Louie from behind. We weren't about to let that happen."

"Yes, yes." Jeff nodded sadly. "A terrible misunderstanding. You can be sure I'll be talking to these boys about it." With a small wave of his hand he dismissed the two bartenders.

When he looked back at the Hardys, he was all smiles. "Please," he said. "Enjoy lunch on the house. My compliments." Still smiling, he turned and headed back to the kitchen.

Nancy gave Frank a quick look. "Weird guy," she said in a low voice.

Frank nodded. "I know. I mean, Joe and I just trashed his place," he said, completing Nancy's thought. "Why would he buy us lunch?"

"Maybe he's just trying not to cause trouble," Joe suggested. "From the look of it, the last thing he needs is bad publicity."

"Yeah," said Bess. She had come over from the booth to join them. "But how much publicity can we create? We're not from Memphis."

"Beats me," Joe said, shrugging. "Anyway, we might as well enjoy the lunch."

"How about it, Louie?" Nancy asked, raising her voice and turning to him. "Want to join us for lunch?"

"Are you kidding?" Louie scoffed. "You think I want to eat the slop they serve at this place? Jefferson Eliot had better watch out," Louie grumbled. "I won't stand for his tricks. He's been putting up his posters over mine. He's been bad-mouthing my place. As if he had a leg to stand on!"

As Nancy listened to him complain, she thought of trying to question Louie to see if he might be the Swallow's contact. But seeing his disgruntled expression, she thought better of it. Questioning him when he was in such a bad mood would only put him on the defensive.

Still, there was the question of Beau, too. "Louie," Nancy began, "I wanted to ask you a few questions about the guitar theft."

He looked at her sharply. "What do you have to do with that?"

"I guess I'm just an interested observer," Nancy replied carefully.

"Then you'd better stay out of it." Louie waved her away. "The police are dealing with it. They'll have that drifter before long."

He's so convinced that Beau's guilty, Nancy thought to herself, that he won't even consider any other possibility. "Excuse me," she said aloud, holding up a hand. "You don't know that Beau stole the guitar."

"I know as much as I need to," said Louie. "Now, if you don't mind, I'll be on my way." He was about to leave when his gaze lingered on Joe, as if he'd only just recognized him.

"You're the one my daughter's been dating," he said.

Louie's statement seemed like an exaggeration to Nancy, considering Joe had only spent one evening on the town with Jennifer.

Joe shrugged, looking slightly embarrassed. "Yeah," he said. "I guess so."

"You're all right," said Louie. His mouth curved up in an approving smile. "Thank you for helping me out here." Then he strode out of the restaurant.

"I never thought I'd say this, but maybe we

should skip the free lunch," Bess suggested. "That Jeff Eliot gives me the creeps."

"I'm with you," Joe agreed. "I don't trust a guy who smiles one second and sends his thugs after you the next. We're out of here."

The four teens headed out to the red convertible, drove back to the Peabody, and parked in the hotel's parking lot.

The first person Joe saw when they reached the entrance was Jennifer Pardee. She was coming out of the hotel.

When she saw Joe, her face lit up. "Well, if it isn't Joe Hardy," she said. "I'm so glad to see you."

Joe broke into a wide grin. "Hey there, Jennifer," he greeted her. "What's happening?"

"That's just what I want to know. I've been here at the hotel hoping to see you again. I still have to take you to Graceland, after all. Where have you been?"

"Well," said Joe. "I have a terrible confession to make. We just went to the Rock Spot."

"You didn't!" Jennifer teased.

"Guilty," Joe said, laughing. "But we never did eat. Your father showed up as well."

"My father?" Jennifer instantly looked concerned. "What was he doing there?"

"Just registering a complaint with the management," Joe told her.

"And getting into hot water," added Bess. "Frank and Joe pulled him out of it, though."

"What?" Jennifer looked totally confused.

"Oh, it wasn't so bad." Joe shrugged modestly. "Just a misunderstanding that got a bit rough. But your dad's fine, and so are we."

"I was talking to that Beau guy," said Jennifer. "And he told me that you all are detectives."

"Sort of," Joe admitted uneasily.

Nancy exchanged a quick look with the Hardys. Why hadn't they warned Beau to keep quiet about their investigation? she thought. Jennifer could be the daughter of the Swallow's contact. If Louie *was* the contact, and he found out about their case, there was no telling what he'd do.

"Investigating sounds so thrilling," Jennifer said, excited. "Tell me, what's it like? What are you doing in Memphis?"

"We're on vacation," Frank said. "We're just enjoying the sights."

Nancy could tell Frank was thinking the same thing she was.

"Oh, I don't believe that," Jennifer said with a sly grin. She placed her hand on Joe's arm. "What are you looking for?"

"Really," Joe told her. "Nothing. We're taking a break." He had recovered his composure and shot her a dazzling grin.

"I don't believe that for one minute," Jennifer repeated. She seemed to be perfectly at ease. Yet Nancy wondered if there was some special reason she kept pressing the issue.

"Maybe we should all go into the hotel instead of standing around out here," Nancy suggested. They all started moving to the entrance.

Letting Joe and Jennifer pass through the doors first, Nancy whispered to Frank, "She's asking an awful lot of questions."

"You think she's pumping Joe for information?" Frank asked.

"It's hard to tell," Nancy replied.

Frank's face tensed. "It's possible that someone's onto us."

"Jennifer *is* Louie's daughter," Nancy pointed out. "And Louie is one of our suspects—he could be the Swallow's contact."

"It's worth keeping in mind," Frank agreed. "I just hope Joe's not getting into something he's going to regret."

Nancy looked into the lobby to where Joe and Jennifer were standing. They were nodding and laughing. Every now and then Jennifer would place a hand on his arm and leave it there for a moment. Joe was clearly enjoying every second with her.

With a sigh Nancy followed Frank and Bess over to the couple.

"Uh, Joe," said Frank. His brother and Jennifer turned toward him. "Don't forget we have to wait for that call in our room."

Joe gave him a dazed look. "Huh?"

"You remember, to confirm your travel plans for the flight back home," Nancy prompted, hoping Joe would realize they had to discuss the case.

"Oh, yeah," said Joe. "Right." He turned to Jennifer. "Sorry, but we've got to take care of this."

"Okay," she said. "That's just as well. I've got to be going myself. But I hope you're not leaving too soon." Giving Joe a flirtatious smile, and the rest of the gang a wave, she left the hotel.

"Wow," said Joe, a huge grin covering his face. "She's something else."

"Something else is right," Frank muttered. "Something other than this case. It's time for us to get down to business. Why don't we head upstairs and order room service while we figure out our next move?"

"Sounds like a good idea," said Nancy, but she noticed that Bess was biting her lip. "Is something wrong, Bess?" Nancy asked.

"Well," Bess began hesitantly, "would you guys mind if I took the afternoon off from the case? I mean, if you want me to help, I will, but I saw the greatest-looking stores when Joe and Frank and I went to get the car. I'm dying to get some shopping in."

Nancy laughed. "We'll be fine. Go for it, Bess."

Twenty minutes later Nancy and the Hardys were in the boys' room munching on sandwiches and drinking sodas they had ordered from room service.

"So, what's next?" asked Nancy, taking a bite of her egg salad sandwich.

"Like you said before, I think we'd better check out Jack Arvis before he leaves town tomorrow," said Frank. "At this point I think he's our most likely suspect." He put his roast beef sandwich down to take a gulp of soda.

"Right," Joe agreed. "Ernest Teague is out with a broken leg, and Bill Cooper seems to be sticking around town. We don't know about Louie yet—we'll have to find out his plans. That's everyone, isn't it?"

"As far as we know," said Frank. "So it seems like the next logical move is for us to check out Arvis and Louie. Let's try Arvis first, since he works right here in the hotel."

"Good idea," said Nancy. "We'll find out from Beau where he is, then see what he has to say."

Just then the phone rang. Frank picked it up.

"Hello?" he said. After a moment his eyes widened. Gesturing to Joe and Nancy, he mouthed the name "Pritchitt."

Instantly both Nancy and Joe were at Frank's side. He bent the receiver away from his ear so they could all hear.

"They got me," Pritchitt was saying. "They were onto me, came to the hotel. That's why I changed the meeting place." He was talking in a rush and keeping his voice low. "I thought I could give them the slip. But they must have followed me to Louie's. When I spotted them, I ran for it, but they shot at me. Then they caught up to me in my truck."

So *that* was what had happened, Nancy thought. Whoever had kidnapped Pritchitt must have been holding him captive in the red pickup truck last night when they saw it.

Frank was frowning. "Where are you now?" he said into the phone. *"Who* got you?"

"I managed to escape. I didn't tell them anything. Now, listen, I left the information for you."

"Where?" Frank asked urgently. "We didn't get it."

"I left it for you," said Pritchitt. "It's—"

All of a sudden there was a sickening thud. The muffled sound of someone talking in a foreign language came out of the phone.

Then the line went dead.

Chapter

Eight

T HAT MUST BE KLAUS!" Frank said, slamming down the phone. "Or one of his men." He felt a sick feeling in his gut. "I couldn't hear his voice that clearly, but he was speaking German. Klaus has Pritchitt."

"Yeah," said Joe. "It sounds like Pritchitt's in big trouble." He began to pace worriedly.

Nancy sat back down on one of the beds. "So now we know there are at least two of Klaus's agents here—the guy Joe saw in the sedan with the blond crew cut and the scar on his lip, and whoever was holding Pritchitt in his pickup." She looked at Frank. "Or do you think one of them was Klaus himself?"

Frank shook his head. "Probably not," he said. "A superspy like Klaus would have his henchmen do the dirty work. It's more likely that those guys are Klaus's agents."

Frank was thinking about the thud they'd heard over the phone. "Listen, guys," he went on. "It sounded like Klaus's men hurt Pritchitt. He said he didn't tell them anything before he escaped. But now that they have him again, who knows what Klaus will do to make Pritchitt talk? He could find out who the Swallow's contact is at any moment."

"Which means we've got to get to the contact first," Nancy said.

"And we still don't know who it is!" Joe was still pacing, and his fists were clenched at his sides.

Frank took a few deep breaths, forcing himself to think calmly. "Pritchitt said he left the information for us," he reasoned. "Which means that he expected us to be able to find it. We've just got to figure out where."

"There were no messages or packages left for us at the desk downstairs," Joe said.

"And we didn't find anything conclusive at Pritchitt's house," Nancy added.

Frank thought for a bit. "Hey! Maybe he left the information at Left-Hand Louie's somewhere. That's where we were supposed to meet him. He probably had the package with him there. I bet he got rid of it when he saw that Klaus's goons were onto him."

Joe nodded eagerly. "That's got to be it! Let's get over there right away."

"Wait a second," Frank said, putting a hand up. As always, Joe couldn't stand to remain still. "If Arvis is really our man, we want to get to him before Klaus finds out his identity from Pritchitt."

"We'd better find him first," Nancy agreed. "If we're wrong, we can go to Louie's right afterward."

"Check," said Joe. "You know, there's something else that bothers me."

"What's that?" Frank asked.

Joe's blue eyes looked steadily at Frank. "If Pritchitt was being held captive last night, who stole our money?"

"Do you think it was Klaus?" Nancy asked.

Joe shrugged. "But how could he have gotten onto us so quickly?"

Frank had been asking himself the same question, and he didn't like the answer he came up with.

Shooting a serious glance at the others, he said, "Remember, Grady thought there was a double agent in the Network. Klaus probably knew we were coming before *we* knew. The agent's identity is one of the secrets the Swallow is supposed to have. Can you imagine? If a traitor could have caused us this much trouble on a simple courier job, imagine how much trouble he could cause on missions of vital national security."

"I'd say that makes this mission one of vital national security," Nancy said quietly. "This isn't just a courier job anymore."

For a moment no one said anything. Then Frank broke the silence. "We should get going."

Suddenly there was a knock on the door.

"Shh," said Frank, leaping up from the bed. He went to the door and said, "Who is it?"

The response was muffled. Frank slid the re-straining chain into its slot and carefully opened the door a crack.

"Beau." Frank didn't know whether to be relieved or annoyed.

"Hi," he said. "I'm looking for Nancy."

Letting out a breath, Frank took the chain off and let the door swing open. "She's here," he said.

"Howdy." Beau waved to Nancy and Joe as he entered the room.

"Hi, Beau," said Nancy.

Beau looked uneasily back and forth between Frank and Joe. From the look on his face, Frank guessed he wanted to talk to Nancy alone. "Why don't Joe and I go downstairs and wait for you?" he suggested, flipping Nancy the key to the room. He followed Joe out the door.

"See you in a few," Joe called over his shoulder.

"What is it?" Nancy asked when she and Beau were alone.

"Well, um," Beau stammered. "Do you have any leads on who stole Louie's guitar?"

"Not yet," she told him. "We've been pretty busy with something else. But we'll get to it," she promised.

"Uh-huh," said Beau. Nancy didn't think the guitar was the real reason Beau wanted to talk to her. Besides, she thought, he could easily have asked about the guitar in front of Frank and Joe. They were working on that case, too.

Nancy gave him a questioning look. "Is something else on your mind, Beau?" she asked.

He was silent for a second. Then he blurted out, "It's Bess."

Nancy blinked. "Yes?"

"I just passed her in the lobby," Beau continued. "I guess she was on her way out to go shopping or something. She's the greatest."

Nancy grinned. She liked Beau's open appreciation. Bess *was* the greatest. However, she already had a boyfriend.

"Well, I was kind of wondering," Beau went on. "One minute she seems to like me, and the next she hardly even notices me. Like last night. I had the feeling she really wanted me to come along with you guys, after we left Louie's. But when I saw her just now, she walked right by me without saying hello. I don't get it. Is she mad at me for going to Sun Studios instead of joining you?"

Nancy could understand why Beau would be confused. Bess seemed to be flip-flopping between flirting with him and remaining true to Craig.

"I'm sure she's not angry, Beau," Nancy said truthfully. "And I know she thinks you're nice." Nancy hesitated. It wasn't up to her to tell him about Bess's private affairs. "I doubt she's being rude on purpose. It's just that we're only here for a week, and there's so much to see and do." Not to mention a case to solve, she added to herself.

Beau smiled, seeming satisfied with the explanation. "Yeah, you're right. So it's not that she minds my company."

"Not at all," Nancy told Beau truthfully. She could tell Bess really liked Beau. Bess would just have to decide for herself whether she wanted to do anything about it.

Beau was about to leave when Nancy said, "Oh, by the way, do you know where Jack Arvis is?"

He nodded. "Usually he's wherever the ducks are," Beau replied. "But today he's at home. He decided to get ready for his trip a day early."

"Can you give me his address?" Nancy asked urgently. She hoped he hadn't already left.

Beau looked a little surprised, but he told Nancy where Arvis lived. After Beau left, Nancy locked the Hardys room, then rode the elevator to the lobby. She glanced around until she found Frank and Joe, standing by the fountain.

Hurrying over to them, she said, "Arvis isn't here. He's at home. I think we'd better go over there right away."

Frank headed for the doors, but Joe caught his older brother's arm.

"Just a minute," Joe said. He was staring at something across the lobby. "Look at that," he said. "It's Jennifer."

Nancy followed his gaze. Sure enough, Jennifer was standing by the bank of telephones, talking to someone on the other end.

"That's funny," Frank said, frowning. "I thought she said earlier that she was leaving."

Oblivious of his brother's comment, Joe raised his hand and waved eagerly until Jennifer noticed him. She gave him a curt wave in response and turned to face the wall, still talking on the phone.

"How do you like that?" said Joe, looking puzzled. "Before she acted like she'd die if she didn't get to see me. Now I feel as if I don't even exist."

Nancy saw the look of concern in Frank's brown eyes. She wondered if he was thinking the same thing she was—Jennifer could be spying on them.

Frowning, Frank said, "Listen, Joe, maybe you

should forget about Jennifer for now." He took a deep breath. "I mean, until we're sure she's not involved in this thing."

"What are you suggesting?" Joe asked defensively.

"Come on, Joe," said Frank. "You know what I'm saying. Jennifer might be spying on us. It's possible Louie really is the Swallow's contact, and she's helping him. Maybe we shouldn't trust Jennifer."

The brothers glared at each other. Nancy could see that neither one of them was going to back down, so she stepped between them.

"It's just something to think about, Joe," Nancy said. "Come on. Let's go cruising in that Jerry Lee Lewis special."

"Yeah, right," Joe answered. But his enthusiasm seemed a bit dampened.

They went to the hotel parking lot and got into the red convertible. Joe started the engine, then pulled out into the street. The stoplight at the first corner was red, and they pulled to a halt.

"Look," said Frank. "There's one of those Delta Ducks." He pointed down the street. Coming toward them was one of the boats on wheels he and Nancy had seen earlier. This one was empty of tourists, though.

"Must have just dropped off a group," said Nancy. "I bet the driver's heading back to the marina."

"Those things are from World War Two," said Frank.

"Ancient history," Joe said. "It's amazing they can still put that old army surplus stuff to use."

"It must be fun riding in one of those up the Mississippi," Nancy commented, still looking at the Duck. "When this case is wrapped up, we should go on one."

"Sure thing," agreed Frank, turning around and smiling at her.

The light turned green. Joe gave the car some gas, and Nancy settled back to enjoy the ride. Suddenly her attention was caught by a familiar figure on the sidewalk.

It was the blond man with the scar.

"Joe, wait!" Nancy yelled. The car jerked to a halt, causing her to lurch forward momentarily.

"What is it?" Joe asked, a hint of alarm in his voice.

"There!" Nancy cried, pointing. "See him? That's the guy who was chasing Pritchitt outside of Louie's!"

The man was just coming out of an alley. Hearing Nancy's shouts, he froze. His eyes met Nancy's for a moment, causing her to shiver down to her toes. Then he burst into a run and took off down the sidewalk.

"We've got to get him!" Nancy cried.

Joe stomped on the gas pedal, and the wheels screeched against the asphalt. Bracing himself on the dashboard, Frank brought his feet up so that he was crouching on the car seat. He was ready to spring out of the car in a second if he had to.

The blond man darted in front of the convertible. He paused briefly to look around, then noticed the Delta Duck, which was still lumbering down the street. Leaping on board, he grabbed the driver by the shirt and hurled him onto the pavement.

The blond man swung the Duck into a broad turn. Nancy heard the driver yell and saw him shake his fist. But it was too late. The blond man shot off in the opposite direction.

Chapter

Nine

Hold on!" Joe called. "I'm going after him." He jerked the steering wheel to the left, and tires screeched as the convertible turned around in a U-turn.

Nancy gripped the seat in front of her, leaning forward so her head was between Frank's and Joe's. Ahead, she saw the Duck bounce up and over the corner of the sidewalk as it veered left, sending pedestrians scurrying for safety.

"This guy's a maniac!" Frank yelled.

"That thing is fast," Nancy said, speaking loudly to be heard above the roaring engine, "but it doesn't take turns very well."

The wheels of another car screeched, and a

horn blared to their right. "Watch it," Nancy warned as Joe swerved. "That was close."

Ahead of them, the Duck careened through another turn, then another. The Duck's driver wasn't worrying about pedestrians. He crashed over sidewalks at full speed. Joe had to slow down at each turn to stay on the road. On straightaways, however, he made up for lost ground.

"I wish I knew this city better," said Joe. "I might be able to cut him off somewhere."

"He doesn't know Memphis too well, either," Nancy reminded him. "Just stick with him."

The two vehicles spun onto Front Street. "A wide street," said Joe. "Watch me catch up to that bozo!" He pumped the gas, and the convertible shot forward.

They were heading north, with the Mississippi River to the west.

"Pull up to his left side," Frank spoke up. "Get between him and the river."

Joe pulled into the left lane, gaining on the Duck. Just as he came even with the back of the vehicle, it swerved to the left, cutting Joe off.

Frank braced himself against the dash as Joe stomped quickly on the brakes, narrowly avoiding a crash. The Duck swung right again.

"Two can play this game." Joe's jaw clenched as he darted the car forward. Again the Duck swung broadside, whipping left immediately in front of the convertible.

"Look out!" cried Nancy.

Frank was thrown against the door as Joe spun the wheel to the left, trying to keep from being hit by the Duck. The two vehicles hit a sharp downhill slope side by side. Looking to the right, Frank got a glimpse of the blond-haired man who was driving the Duck. He stiffened his arms, bracing himself.

The next thing he knew, Nancy was screaming, "Bail out!" Looking ahead, Frank saw that the asphalt sloped right down into the river. The convertible was heading straight for the water, and they were going too fast to stop.

Joe hit the brakes hard, but the car continued to skid toward the river. At the last second Nancy, Frank, and Joe leapt out of the car. They hit the asphalt hard, then rolled to safety, away from both vehicles. Just as Frank looked up, the convertible hit the water with a huge splash, sinking up to the door handles.

At the same time the Delta Duck hit the water with a similar splash. But instead of sinking, it floated safely out into the river. Frank watched in dismay as the Duck's water engines kicked in with a roar, and the spy sailed away. They had lost him.

"Sounds to me like you three were hot-rodding in that flashy car of yours," the police officer scolded as she finished taking a statement from the teenagers. Behind her a tow truck was dragging the convertible out of the water.

As soon as Nancy and the Hardys realized that the blond man with the scar had gotten away, Nancy had found a pay phone and called the police and a towing company. The police officer, a heavyset woman with short blond hair, had arrived soon after. But Joe was having a hard time convincing her that they hadn't been irresponsible.

"Officer," Joe insisted, "you've got to understand. The guy in that Delta Duck ran us off the road. He's a dangerous man."

"Young man," said the officer, "I may let you go with just a warning this time. But get one thing straight. It's up to the police to handle dangerous people. You could get yourself, and others, seriously hurt driving like that."

Nancy could see that Joe was losing his patience. She stepped forward quickly and draped a calming arm around his shoulders. "He'll be careful from now on," she promised the officer. "And thank you for being understanding."

Joe's shoulders were tense, but to Nancy's relief he didn't say anything.

"If it's possible," she continued, "could you radio for a cab? We need to get back to the car-rental agency."

Rather than calling a cab, the police officer drove them herself, all the while lecturing Joe on the importance of driving safely. At the rental agency Joe got a second lecture. Nancy could see that he was about to blow up.

After a bit of persuasion, however, they managed to get a second car—another red convertible—and Joe's good spirits returned.

"Finally," he said, pulling the new car out of the rental lot, "we can visit Jack Arvis."

Nancy pulled out her city map. After spreading it out in the backseat, she plotted the course to Arvis's home. He lived slightly east of midtown, a few miles from the hotel.

His house was a one-story brick building with a wrought-iron railing around the front patio. Several of the surrounding houses were built in a similar style. Joe pulled the convertible up in front, and the three of them got out.

Frank rang the doorbell. Inside, Nancy heard a voice say, "Just a minute." Faint footsteps sounded, and then the door opened.

Nancy recognized the older man from the duck ceremony and Pritchitt's photograph. Arvis stood in a rigid stance as he examined his three visitors, looking down his nose through a pair of bifocals.

"Yes," he said. "What can I do for you?"

"Hi," said Nancy. She introduced herself and Frank and Joe, then said, "We wondered if we could have a word with you."

Frowning, Arvis studied them a moment longer. Then he took a step backward. "Come in," he said.

He led them into a clean, orderly living room. Arvis took the large padded armchair, gesturing them to the sofa. They faced a large television set with framed photographs arranged on top of it.

"We're friends of Hank Pritchitt," Nancy began. She went on to explain that they were staying at the hotel where Pritchitt worked.

Arvis looked at her skeptically. "So? What does that have to do with me?"

"Actually," Nancy improvised, "we came to town to see Pritchitt. We have important family news to give him, but we can't find him anywhere. He hasn't shown up for work, and no one knows where he is." Nancy knew that Frank and Joe would pick up on the story and back her up.

"Not surprising for a fellow like him," said Arvis. "He has a tendency to disappear from time to time. I'm sure *I* don't know where he is."

"Beau Davis said you might be seeing him on Friday night," Nancy said. "He said you get together to play cards."

Arvis narrowed his eyes. "Beau knows better than that. I'm leaving town. Going tomorrow."

"Really?" Joe said. His voice was casual as he asked, "Where are you going?"

"Out of town," Arvis responded.

"Anywhere particular?" Joe pressed.

"Not so it matters to you," Arvis said. "Now, is there anything else? I'm really quite busy."

Jack Arvis sure was being close-mouthed about

the trip, Nancy thought, which wouldn't be surprising if he were the Swallow's contact.

Suddenly her gaze landed on one of the photographs on the television set. It showed a man in a military uniform. He was standing in front of a café in a European town. A sign on the wall behind him was written in German.

"Who's that?" she asked, pointing.

Arvis looked at the picture. "My brother."

"He's in Germany?" Nancy asked.

"He was stationed there," said Arvis. "He's a career military officer." Suddenly he seemed agitated and ill at ease. "Now, see here," he snapped. "Is there anything you want, or are you just wasting my time?"

"Please," said Frank. "We're just trying to track down Mr. Pritchitt."

"Well, I have as little to do with Hank Pritchitt as possible," Arvis retorted. "And I'd advise you to do the same."

Nancy frowned. They obviously weren't going to get any more information out of Arvis. Getting up from her chair, Nancy told the older man, "Sorry to have bothered you."

Frank and Joe stood up, too. Arvis said nothing as they left, just gave them a curt nod.

"He's got to be our man," Joe declared once they were back in the car. "He wouldn't volunteer any information, and he was downright hostile on the subject of Pritchitt."

Nancy nodded. "If Pritchitt is Arvis's poker buddy, and probably a friend, why would he be so down on him?"

"Maybe Arvis had something to do with Pritchitt's disappearance," Joe suggested.

Frank shook his head. "But those guys we heard over the phone sounded German. They were probably Klaus's guys. Arvis doesn't have an accent. Still, we should definitely tail him, starting tomorrow morning. If he is the contact, he'll take us right to the rendezvous with the Swallow."

"My guess is that his brother could be the Swallow," Nancy added excitedly. "Did you get a good look at the picture that was taken in Germany?"

"Yeah. Looked kind of old, though," Joe pointed out.

"True," Nancy said. "But the Swallow's been in Germany for ten years." She tapped her fingers on the car seat, thinking. "Arvis seems like a good bet for the Swallow's contact. But I think we need to consider all of our suspects. We still don't know about Louie."

"That's right," Frank agreed. He hesitated for a moment before adding, "Or Jennifer. We should keep an eye on her, too."

"No way is she mixed up with this," Joe said adamantly. "You're just jealous, big brother, that you don't have my magnetic appeal."

Frank didn't say anything, just rolled his eyes.

Nancy could see that he wanted to avoid another discussion about Jennifer. Nancy just hoped Joe's personal feelings about Jennifer wouldn't get in the way of the case.

"We should get back to the hotel," she said, changing the subject. "Bess will be looking for us. We'll pick her up and get some dinner at Louie's. We can look around for the information Pritchitt said he left us while we're there."

A short while later the four teenagers were seated at a table at Louie's.

"Nice dress," Joe commented, giving Bess a wink. She was wearing the bright blue dress she'd bought that afternoon. Bess appreciated the compliment but could see that Joe's gaze kept searching through the restaurant—no doubt looking for Jennifer.

When the waitress came to take their order, Nancy asked if they could speak to Louie.

Apologetically the waitress said, "I'm afraid I haven't seen him at all tonight."

"Let us know if he shows up," Frank asked.

The waitress assured them she would. After she had taken their orders and left, Frank leaned close to the others and said, "I don't like this. What if Louie's already left for the Gulf of Mexico?"

"I doubt he would have left for a few days without telling the people in his restaurant," Nancy replied. "He'll probably be back soon."

But when the group had finished eating, Louie still hadn't appeared. They looked around as inconspicuously as possible for the information Pritchitt had left but found nothing.

By the time they were ready to return to the hotel, Nancy was wondering if they were ever going to come up with a solid lead in this case.

Early the next morning, while Bess was still asleep, Nancy went down to the lobby to meet the Hardys. They needed to come up with a plan in a hurry. It was already Wednesday, and the meeting with the Swallow was supposed to happen Thursday night. Time was running out.

As Nancy spotted the brothers coming out of the elevator, she heard someone call her name. Turning, she saw Tad Baker, waving a note at the front desk. "Message, Ms. Drew."

Nancy took the slip of paper, a note from Beau, and read it. "Need to talk to you ASAP. Meet me at the duck tank."

"Good morning," said Frank, coming up behind Nancy with his brother. "What's that?"

"A message from Beau," Nancy told him. "It doesn't tell me much, just that he wants to meet me upstairs. Maybe he found something out about Pritchitt."

Joe began tapping his foot impatiently. "Well, let's get going."

The three of them caught the elevator up to the top floor, where the duck tank was.

"What a racket," Frank said as they walked down the hallway. "Listen to them squawk."

Walking slightly ahead, Nancy came to a door marked Duck Tank.

"Good thing it's marked," Joe said sarcastically, raising his voice over the quacking. "We'd never have found it otherwise."

The door was slightly ajar. Nancy knocked. "Beau?" she called in a voice she hoped he could hear over the noise. There was no answer.

She pushed the door open and found herself looking into darkness. Feeling along the wall, she found a light switch and flipped it on.

Nancy gasped as she realized with horror why the ducks were quacking so loudly. In their midst, floating facedown in the tank, was a body.

Chapter

Ten

JOE RUSHED PAST NANCY to the duck tank and looked at the body. "It's Pritchitt," he said with a shudder. "And he's dead."

Nancy and Frank came up behind him. For a moment all they could do was stare at Pritchitt's still form.

"How awful," Nancy said at last.

The sound of her voice snapped Joe out of his daze. Turning to the others, he said, "We'd better go get the manager."

"I'll go," Nancy said.

Joe could feel his adrenaline pumping. He was bursting with nervous energy and began pacing uneasily back and forth. "Things are getting worse, Frank. We're down to murder now—and we've lost our best lead."

He glanced at Frank. "How did this happen? I mean, whoever killed him could be right here in the hotel." He paused for a second. "Do you think Klaus did it?"

"Klaus? Maybe," Frank said at last. He was trying to remain clear-headed and calm. "But there are other possibilities. Pritchitt's in the duck tank, which is Jack Arvis's work area. That makes Arvis a suspect, too. If *he's* the Swallow's contact, he had plenty of reasons to hold a grudge against Pritchitt. We still don't know how Louie could fit into the picture, either."

"That's true," Joe said. His hands clenched into fists. "But I bet it was Klaus. Frank, he could have been holding Pritchitt right here in the hotel the whole time! And if he killed Pritchitt, it might mean he got the information he'd wanted and then got rid of him."

"Or maybe Klaus gave up trying," Frank pointed out. "But you're right. Pritchitt could have been here all along. We should question the hotel workers to see if anyone's seen anything suspicious."

"Hey, what about Beau?" Joe asked. "Do you think he really left that message for us?"

Frank thought for a minute. "I doubt it, since he's not here. Looks like someone's setting him up." He frowned. "And whoever it is knows who we all are and what we're investigating."

Shaking his head, Joe said, "It's going to look pretty bad for Beau until we find out who the murderer is."

Just then Nancy returned with the manager, a portly man of about forty with thinning hair and a brown suit. He was panic-stricken by the news of Pritchitt's death. The police—four officers and a rescue squad—followed a few minutes later. They pulled Pritchitt's wet body out of the tank.

The manager wrung his hands and averted his eyes from the body. "I can't believe it," he said. "A person murdered here, and I don't even have my house detective."

"Pritchitt *was* your house detective," Joe pointed out. The manager wasn't thinking too clearly.

One of the officers approached the teenagers and said, "The man's been dead since some time last night. Do you know his name?"

Joe looked at Frank and Nancy, then back at the officer. "Yes," he answered. "His name was Hank Pritchitt."

"Was he a friend of yours?" asked the officer.

"An acquaintance," Joe said curtly.

"But you're from out of town," said the officer. "That seems like an odd coincidence."

Joe hesitated, searching for an answer that

wouldn't give away anything about their case. Luckily, he didn't have to come up with one, because the manager interrupted them.

"Officer," said the manager. He stepped between Joe and the policeman and waved his hand toward the teenagers. "You shouldn't be questioning these kids. You should talk to the duck keeper's assistant, Beau Davis. He was probably the last one to see Hank alive."

The officer jotted something down in his notebook. "Where can we find this Beau Davis?" he asked.

The manager checked his watch. "He'll be here any minute. At ten o'clock he has to bring the ducks downstairs."

"Where's he from?" the officer asked, still writing in his notebook.

"I'm not sure," the manager replied. "I think he's a drifter. I've seen Beau and Pritchitt arguing more than once. And Beau works right here in this room. Not many people have access. Beau has a key."

Nancy stepped forward. "Beau wouldn't kill anyone," she declared.

"You know this Davis fella?" asked the officer.

"Yes," said Nancy.

The officer looked at Joe, then back at Nancy. "You kids seem to know a lot of people involved with this case," he said. "I'll expect you to remain in contact with us. We might want you to answer some questions."

This is bad, Joe thought. A police investigation could get in the way of our search.

The officers took statements from the three teens and got their room numbers. After about half an hour, they were told they could leave, and they headed for the lobby.

"I feel bad leaving before Beau arrives," Nancy said. "He's in for a nasty surprise."

"He can take care of himself," Frank said. "Right now we've got to figure out our next move with the case. I think it's fair to say that things have gotten pretty urgent."

"Nancy!"

They all turned to see Bess hurrying toward them.

"Where have you been?" Bess asked, a look of concern on her face. "I've been waiting here for half an hour."

"I'm sorry, Bess," said Nancy. "With all the excitement, we forgot about meeting for breakfast."

Bess looked from Nancy to the Hardys. "Excitement? What happened?" Her pretty face went pale when Nancy explained about Pritchitt's murder. "Nancy," she said with a gasp. "This is getting dangerous!"

Nancy nodded. "And it gets worse." She told Bess that Beau would most likely be one of the police's suspects for the murder. "They're probably going to be pretty rough on him. I bet he'd appreciate it if you'd wait here for him after he brings the ducks down. Make sure he's all right, would you mind?" Nancy asked her friend.

"The poor guy," Bess said. "Of course I'll stay."

"See, Bess, detective work isn't all that bad. You get to hang around with a cute guy."

"I could get to like this," Bess said with a laugh.

Nancy gave her friend a quick hug. "Thanks, Bess," she said. She turned to the Hardys. "Well," she asked. "Where to?"

Frank gave it a moment's thought. Then he said, "Arvis. He's leaving on his trip today, and we've got to trail him. The way I see it, either Arvis or Klaus killed Pritchitt. If we tell Arvis that Pritchitt's dead and we know he's the Swallow's contact, Arvis is likely to come clean. It's the best shot we have at the moment."

Joe agreed. They got in the red convertible in the hotel's parking lot and drove to Arvis's house. When they arrived, Joe noticed that Arvis's car was still in the driveway. "Good," he said, pointing to it. "He hasn't left yet."

They rang the doorbell and waited. There was no response. They rang it again, following with a knock. Still no response.

"That's odd," said Nancy, sounding worried.

"Hmm. Wait a minute," said Joe. He stepped

off the porch and walked along the side of the house to a window. From their visit the day before, he guessed it was the living room window. Cupping his hands above his eyes, he peered inside. The room looked pretty much the same. He studied it carefully, looking for anything out of place.

Then he noticed that two of the photographs on top of the television had been knocked over. It wasn't like Arvis, who had seemed so neat and orderly, to leave a mess like that.

Joe walked around to the back of the house with a sense of building urgency. Stopping at another window, higher up, Joe stood on his toes and looked inside.

The first thing his gaze landed on was the refrigerator and stove, with striped wallpaper behind them. Then Joe felt his blood pounding as he saw something else. Jack Arvis was tied to a kitchen chair, gagged and blindfolded.

"Guys!" Joe yelled. "It's Arvis! He's tied up."

The others were beside him in a flash. Joe tried the back door and found it unlocked. He rushed inside, with Frank and Nancy a step behind him.

"Are you all right?" Joe asked, pulling off Arvis's gag and blindfold.

Arvis gasped, breathing deeply. "Hurry up, untie me," he growled. "I've been like this half the night and all morning."

"What happened?" Frank asked him.

"Some crazy couple broke in here last night," said Arvis. "Tied me up and started ranting."

"A couple?" asked Nancy.

"Man and a woman," Arvis said as Joe bent to untie the ropes around the older man's wrists. "Man tied me up. Ugly-looking blond guy. Nasty scar on his face. The woman did all the talking, though I didn't get to see her."

"Mr. Arvis," Frank said, "it's time we leveled with you. We know you're the contact. We know your brother's the Swallow."

Arvis exploded. "That's just what the woman kept saying!" he yelled. "What's going on here?"

Joe finished untying the rope around Arvis's ankles. He looked up into Arvis's eyes and said, "Pritchitt is dead."

"What?" Arvis's eyes widened. "Hank Pritchitt is dead? How did that happen?"

"He was killed last night," Nancy explained. "At least, we think it happened then. We found him this morning at the Peabody."

"Why . . ." Arvis seemed stunned. "I guess an operator like Pritchitt was bound to come into some trouble. But—someone *killed* him?" Arvis shivered in fear.

"Listen," said Frank. "You're going out of town today. We know you're going to visit your brother."

"That's right," said Arvis, still dazed. "How did you know that?"

"We know all about it," Joe burst out impatiently. "He's coming in from Berlin sometime before tomorrow night. You're meeting him at the Gulf of Mexico."

"The Gulf of Mexico?" exclaimed Arvis. "Berlin? My brother hasn't been in Germany for fifteen years. And that was Munich."

Nancy blinked in surprise. "What?"

"I'm going to Marked Tree, Arkansas. That's where my brother has been ever since he retired. You can call him and ask him yourself."

Nancy could tell by the looks on the Hardy brothers' faces that they were as stunned as she was.

"Why were you so secretive about your trip?" Frank asked.

Arvis looked down. "I'm not very proud about begging my own brother for money," he said. "Fact is, my old buddy Pritchitt talked me into an investment deal that went sour. You don't need to know the details. I owe the bank a tidy sum, and I was hoping my brother could help me out."

There was sadness and sincerity in his voice. Nancy felt sure that he was telling the truth. No wonder he'd spoken so angrily of Hank Pritchitt yesterday, she thought.

Jack Arvis wasn't their man, she realized with

a sigh. She and the Hardys had wasted all this valuable time on the wrong track. They still had no idea who it was they were looking for. And the real contact could be leaving Memphis at any moment for tomorrow's meeting on the Gulf of Mexico.

Chapter

Eleven

I DON'T BELIEVE THIS," Frank said. He looked at Joe and Nancy, who were leaning against the counter in Arvis's kitchen. "We're back to square one."

"Not quite," Nancy pointed out. If Arvis wasn't the Swallow's contact, she was thinking, at least he might be able to give us some information. "What can you tell us about the people who tied you up?" she asked.

Arvis scratched his head. "The man's easy to describe, because he's so ugly. And he had that scar. But the woman, well—" He shrugged.

"What did her voice sound like?" Frank prompted.

Arvis thought for a moment. "She had a funny accent," he said. "I can't really place it, though."

"A German accent?" Joe asked.

"I don't think so," Arvis responded, shaking his head. "Not so as you'd notice it. I just know it wasn't a southern accent."

Nancy knit her brow in concentration. She could think of one person whose voice fit that description—Tracy Brandt. The woman had been present at Louie's that first night, and she had spent time at the hotel. Nancy shook herself. What was she thinking? That was hardly a reason to suspect Ms. Brandt of any wrongdoing. Still, if she saw her again, it couldn't hurt to ask a few questions.

Nancy saw Arvis check his watch. "Well, I don't know what you kids are up to," Arvis said, "but I've got to get going."

Joe's mouth dropped open. "You're not still making the trip, are you?"

"Of course I am," said Arvis matter-of-factly.

"Don't you want to find the people who tied you up?" Joe pressed, incredulous.

"It can wait," said Arvis. "The banks won't. At my age that's one lesson I've learned."

Nancy had to admit Arvis had a point. "I'm afraid we might not be here by the time you get back," she told him. "But we'll still work on the case in your absence."

Arvis nodded. "Now, if you'll excuse me," he said, "I need to finish packing."

After saying goodbye, Nancy, Frank, and Joe left. They piled into the convertible and started driving back toward downtown.

"We still don't know who the contact is," said Frank after a short silence. "We're running out of time."

Joe turned to look at his brother in the passenger seat. "At least we've got the field narrowed down," he pointed out. "Assuming the contact is one of Pritchitt's former poker buddies, it seems like we're down to Bill Cooper and Louie Pardee."

Nancy nodded. "Bill Cooper claimed he'd be in town Thursday night. I guess he could have been lying, but I don't know why he'd think he had to. I wasn't obvious about asking."

"So I guess Louie is our prime suspect," Frank concluded. He slapped his brother on the shoulder and instructed, "Next stop—Left-Hand Louie's."

Louie's wasn't as crowded as the other two times Nancy and the others had been there. But it was still early, she reminded herself, and there was no band playing. A lunchtime crowd was beginning to gather.

As soon as he entered the restaurant, Joe started looking around. He was trying to be casual, but Nancy knew he was looking for Jennifer. She wasn't there, however.

"Three for lunch?" asked a waiter, approaching them.

"Yes," said Frank. After the waiter had shown them to a table and taken their orders, Frank said to him, "We're hoping to see Louie. Is he around?"

Nancy held her breath. What if he still wasn't there? What if he'd already left for his rendezvous somewhere on the Gulf of Mexico?

"He's in the back," said the waiter. "I'll go get him." Nancy let out a sigh of relief.

Louie came walking out of the kitchen at the same time the waiter brought the teenagers their burgers and sodas. He was rubbing his hands on his apron. He gave Nancy and the Hardys a questioning look, then smiled in recognition.

"Hey," he said, moving forward. "It's my young protectors." He sat down next to Joe and held out his hand. Joe shook it. "How've you been?" Louie asked Joe.

"Fine."

"Are you enjoying your visit?" Louie asked, grinning. "Is Jennifer showing you all the sights?"

"Well, not exactly," said Joe. He frowned slightly.

"You seem like a good fellow," said Louie. "I'm glad to see Jennifer spending her time with you."

Joe laughed, looking slightly embarrassed.

"Well, she hardly spends any time with me," he said. "I've been pretty busy."

Louie didn't seem to hear him. He gave Joe a conspiratorial look, saying, "I must tell you I'm pleased to have you around. Keeps Jennifer's attentions away from where they shouldn't be. You seem like a good fellow." He leaned forward. "Tell me, what are your plans?"

Joe's face reddened, and he was obviously uncomfortable under Louie's scrutiny. He looked to his brother for help, but Frank just stretched out his lean frame in his chair and grinned. With a wink at Nancy, Frank said, "Yeah, Joe, have you set the date yet?"

Joe scowled at his brother. Turning back to Louie, he said, "Uh, that's not really what we're here for. We wanted to ask you some questions."

Louie nodded. "Shoot."

"Well, we were just wondering, are you going to be around for the next couple of days?"

"Far as I know," Louie replied.

"Thursday?" Joe asked. "Will you be here on Thursday night?"

"Sure," said Louie. "Are you looking to make reservations?"

"Yes," Frank cut in. "Hank Pritchitt, a guy at our hotel, said this place is always more lively when you're around." He hesitated before asking, "Do you know Pritchitt?"

Louie's eyes narrowed. "We're friends," he said. "We play cards together. Why?"

"He was in here the other day," said Nancy. "The day Beau Davis played your guitar. He was waiting to meet some people."

"Yes, I saw him." Louie's face was guarded. "So?"

"We're the guys he was going to meet," Frank said. "Only something happened. Someone else showed up and chased him off."

"So he was there when the shots rang out, huh? Pretty wild story." Louie's voice was guarded. He studied the group.

Nancy felt herself growing impatient. They didn't have time to waste with this kind of verbal jousting. She decided to try for some shock value. "The same people who chased him off caught up with him last night. They killed him."

Louie was plainly stunned. "Killed him? Who did it?"

"We're not sure," Nancy replied. "But we think the murderer was after the same information Pritchitt was going to give us."

"What information?" asked Louie.

If Louie was bluffing, he was doing a good job. Still, Nancy couldn't rule out the possibility that he was just covering up his knowledge of the information packet. She pressed him further. "He told us he left some information for us. We assume he left it here."

"Well, he didn't tell me about it." Louie shook his head, his eyes still wide open. "Hank is dead? I just can't believe it."

"It's important information," Frank said. "Do you know where he might have left it?"

Louie shook his head. "He knew the place pretty well. And everyone who works here knew him. He used to talk to all of us. I can't say I saw him anywhere in particular. It could be anywhere. How big is it?"

"We don't really know," said Nancy. "But it's probably just a photograph, maybe with a note attached."

"You're welcome to look around," said Louie, motioning to the restaurant with his hands.

"We already did," said Frank. "Last night. But we didn't find anything. We were hoping to talk to you about it, but you weren't around. Where were you?"

All at once Louie looked annoyed. "Hey, where a man goes on his own time is nobody else's business."

Nancy didn't know what to make of his sudden bad humor. But she did know one thing: Louie didn't have an alibi for the time of Pritchitt's murder.

Glancing up at the empty stage, Nancy suddenly remembered the other case she was working on. "While we're here," she said to Louie, "there's something else I wanted to talk to you about—your guitar."

"My guitar!" Louie exclaimed angrily. "Have they arrested that hoodlum yet?"

"No," said Nancy. She was becoming impatient with Louie's stubborn attitude. "I don't think Beau did it," she said firmly.

"Don't tell me you're sweet on him," Louie scoffed.

Nancy flushed with anger. "No," she said. "I'm just trying to keep an open mind about this. Isn't there anyone else who might have wanted to steal that guitar?"

"Sure," Louie said without hesitating. "It's a big deal. There are lots of people who want it. I get offers all the time."

"Isn't it possible that one of those people stole it? Or that someone took it out of spite?" Nancy suggested.

Louie frowned. "What do you mean?" he asked.

"For example," Nancy explained, "the day the guitar was stolen you fired a guy who worked here."

"Spence Burbank," he said. "A good-for-nothing bum. He was always breaking things."

"Could he have been out for personal revenge?" Nancy prodded.

"You know, he could have," said Louie. "He very well could have." He looked as if a light was dawning on him. "Now that you mention Spence, I believe that's a strong possibility."

Oh, brother, Nancy thought. Louie's suspicion of Spence was just as irrational as his accusation of Beau had been. But at least maybe he would ease up on Beau now.

Suddenly Nancy cocked her head to the side and sniffed. "Is something burning in the kitchen?"

Then she noticed something through the window. A dark cloud of smoke drifted by, followed by another.

"Hey, guys." She got their attention and pointed. "Look out the window." The smoke was stronger now, coming in thick, dark clouds.

Frank jumped to his feet. "Louie," he said urgently, "do you have a chimney or an exhaust vent back there?"

"No," said Louie. "Those go out the roof."

Nancy looked from Frank to Joe. Instantly the three teenagers darted for the door. They ran outside and headed for the back of the restaurant.

Joe was the first to see the fire raging in the garbage Dumpster. The flames shot up the side of the building, reaching for the wooden beams of the overhanging roof.

In a moment the whole building would go up in flames!

Chapter

Twelve

"QUICK!" Nancy shouted to the Hardys. "Get some fire extinguishers. And tell someone to call the fire department."

While Frank and Joe dashed back into the restaurant, Nancy looked hurriedly around for something she could use to fight the blaze. Spotting a hose connected to an outdoor faucet, she ran over to it and picked it up. As she did so, Louie rushed out of the restaurant.

"That Dumpster is full of grease," he said when he saw Nancy with the hose. "Water won't be much help."

"That's okay," she told him. She turned on the faucet and started spraying the roof beams. "If I can keep the wood wet, the roof might not catch fire." Seeing the helpless look on Louie's face, she shouted over to him, "Call the fire department."

Frank and Joe burst out of the restaurant a moment later, each carrying a fire extinguisher. They ran up to the Dumpster but were repelled by the intense heat of the fire.

"Spray from a distance," Frank called out.

The two of them advanced on the fire behind a cloud of white foam. Finally they got close enough to spray directly into the Dumpster. The fire was stubborn, though, and kept burning through the onslaught of foam. The thick smoke stung their eyes, and all three teenagers were coughing.

"This thing won't go out!" Joe called.

"Louie was right!" Nancy yelled to the Hardys. "The Dumpster is filled with grease from frying. It's like a giant torch."

At last the flames subsided. Nancy turned off the water hose, and she, Frank, and Joe collapsed on the ground. In the distance they heard the wail of fire engines.

"It's a good thing we didn't wait for the fire department," she said, looking up at the soot-blackened roof beams. "If that fire had spread to the roof, Louie's would have been history."

Frank wiped his soot-blackened brow with the back of his hand. "Do you think someone set this fire?" he asked.

"I wouldn't be surprised," Nancy told him.

Joe jumped to his feet. "Let's see if there are any clues," he suggested.

They were busy scouring the ground near the Dumpster when Louie came out of the restaurant.

"Thank you," Louie said, going over to them. "I can't thank you enough. It just makes me sick to think of what could have happened. Are you all right?"

Nancy assured Louie that she and the Hardys were not harmed, then leveled a serious gaze at him. "Do you think this was an accident?" she said.

"What do you mean?" Louie asked.

"Well," Nancy said, "first your famous guitar is stolen. Now we have a fire that could easily have burned your place to the ground. This may be a case of arson."

Louie nodded grimly. "I see what you mean," he said. "I bet it was Spence Burbank."

Louie was jumping to conclusions again, Nancy thought. "We won't know who it was until we find some proof," she told him. "But Spence *is* a possibility."

"Hey, look at this!"

Turning, Nancy saw that Joe was holding something shiny and studying it. "What's that?" she asked.

Joe held it up. "I'm not sure. I found it on the

ground." He was holding a brass cylinder, about an inch long and closed at one end.

"That's an odd-looking thing," said Nancy, taking the cylinder from him. It was warm from the fire. A little larger than a thimble, it could have been the top of a fancy perfume bottle—not like anything Nancy would associate with a restaurant.

"It doesn't look like much," said Frank, looking over her shoulder. "But we'd better keep it for now. You never know."

Nancy nodded, handing the brass cylinder to Frank.

Louie looked at the teenagers expectantly. "I assume you're going to set the authorities on Spence Burbank's trail."

"We'll need more proof," Nancy reminded him. "But we'll do our best to find the arsonist."

They said goodbye and left Louie's.

Getting into the car, Frank said, "We can't waste time checking out Spence Burbank. We've got an international spy case to solve."

"And absolutely no leads," Nancy added. "I don't know. Louie acted as if he really didn't know anything about Pritchitt, but he didn't have an alibi for last night."

Joe looked as if he were going to burst from frustration. "But how can we check him out? I mean, we can suspect him all we want, but that still doesn't give us any proof."

"Spence Burbank," Nancy replied. When both Hardys stared at her, she explained. "He used to work at Louie's. Maybe he saw something suspicious that would indicate that Louie is the Swallow's contact."

Frank looked dubious. "It's a long shot, but I guess it's worth a try. We sure don't have any other leads."

"Okay. He's probably at his job over at the Rock Spot," said Nancy.

"Oh, great," Joe said as he drove to the Pyramid. "My favorite place."

As he pulled into the parking lot, Joe looked up at the huge steel pyramid gleaming in the sunlight. "You know, I can't help being impressed every time I see this thing," he admitted. "Can you imagine watching a basketball game in it? Or a rock concert? It would be wild."

Joe pointed to one of the inclined elevators climbing up a corner of the Pyramid. "And riding one of those up to the observation deck. That's something I've definitely got to do before we leave Memphis."

Nancy laughed. "You're just like a kid," she teased. "Don't worry. You'll get a chance to ride up the elevators."

"Come on, Nancy," Joe went on excitedly. "How many elevators do you know that rise at an angle?"

"Well," said Nancy. "There's the Eiffel Tower."

"Exactly," said Joe. "Next best thing to Paris is right here."

They all laughed and climbed out of the car. Inside the Rock Spot there were just two tables occupied. Spence Burbank was sitting behind the cash register, leaning back on a stool. He was wearing headphones and bobbing his head to the music. Realizing some customers had entered the restaurant, Spence whipped off the earphones and jumped to his feet.

"Table for three?" he asked in a southern drawl. Then he did a double take. "Say, aren't you the guys who were in that big fight yesterday?"

"We just stopped by for something to drink," said Nancy, smiling sweetly. "We wanted to make up for our bad behavior by being model customers today."

"Oh, yeah? Right this way." He showed them to a table.

"Didn't you once work at Left-Hand Louie's?" Nancy asked casually as she sat down. "I seem to remember seeing you there." She studied his face, looking for any nervous reaction as she spoke.

"I did—till I was fired," Spence said. He didn't seem concerned about it at all.

"Didn't that make you kind of angry?" Nancy

prompted, hoping to get more of a response from him.

Spence shrugged. "Hey, it was a job. Louie didn't like my work, so he fired me. No big deal." Spence grinned. "I got another job right away, as you can see. And let me tell you, this one is much better."

"How's that?" Frank inquired.

"Easier," said Spence. He leaned forward, speaking in a confidential tone. "To begin with, the Spot is nowhere near as crowded as Louie's. I mean, with so many people in the place asking for this and that and the other, anyone would go crazy. So I dropped a plate or two. What do you expect?

"And another thing," he continued. "My boss, Mr. Eliot, is so much more easygoing than Louie."

"How so?" asked Nancy.

"Well, I mean, Louie was real bosslike. It was his place, you know. No question about that. But he lorded over everything, always making you do this and that. Mr. Eliot helps out a lot. I don't even know what the supply room looks like. He always insists on going and getting supplies himself. Says I should stay out here to make sure the customers have everything they need." He leaned back with a satisfied grin. "That's my kind of boss."

Nancy had to suppress a smile. Obviously,

Spence's idea of a great job was one where he didn't have to do any work. She asked him again about Louie's habits at the restaurant, but Spence didn't have any more to add.

"Have you been here long today?" Nancy asked.

"Yeah," said Spence. He sighed wearily. "Been here since nine o'clock this morning. That's when my shift starts."

Nancy felt a stab of disappointment. That meant Spence couldn't have set the fire at Louie's.

Just then Jeff Eliot came into the restaurant. "Ah," he said. "It's my old sparring partners." He took off his panama hat and placed it on the counter. "Back for a delicious meal, I hope."

Spence said, "I was just telling them what a good boss you are. So much better than Louie."

Jeff laughed. "Everything about this place is better than Louie's. Soon people will realize that." He directed his attention to Nancy. "The Rock Spot will bury Louie's," he said. "You mark my words."

Nancy saw that Joe was glaring at Jeff Eliot. Joe was probably thinking about the way Jeff's thugs had jumped Louie the day before.

"The Rock Spot might do a little better if it didn't try so hard to imitate Louie's," Joe said.

Jeff glared at him. "You're sorely mistaken. Louie's has got nothing on me."

"That's a matter of opinion," Joe retorted.

"Joe," Nancy warned. It wouldn't do them any good to antagonize Jeff this way.

Frank must have been thinking the same thing. Standing up, he nudged his younger brother on the arm and began ushering him toward the exit. "I guess we'll be going now," he said over his shoulder to Jeff.

With an apologetic glance at Jeff, Nancy followed.

"The last thing we need is to make enemies with people," Nancy said to Joe once they were outside. "We don't have many leads on either case, and we need all the help we can get."

"I just don't like Jeff Eliot. Or the way his goons ganged up on Louie," Joe muttered angrily.

"In any case," said Frank, "Nancy's right. We don't need any enemies."

Joe nodded. Taking a deep breath, he admitted, "I guess I'm just frustrated. We're getting nowhere. If Louie is the Swallow's contact, he's not about to admit that to us. Arvis is out. Cooper's working on the night of the meeting. And Teague has a broken leg." He counted the reasons out on his fingers, then threw his arms in the air. "What's left?"

No one answered Joe's question. Nancy knew what the silence was about. They hadn't gotten any closer to finding the Swallow's contact. They couldn't even find the guitar thief.

It was almost Thursday—there were less than thirty-six hours left before the meeting between the Swallow and his contact.

Time was running out!

Chapter
Thirteen

THE GLUM MOOD hung over the three teens as they went back to the hotel. The sun was moving to the west, hanging over the river as they drove toward it. For the first time Nancy noticed what a beautiful, clear, warm day it was.

When they arrived at the Peabody, they parked the car, then circled around to the lobby entrance. As they were heading across the carpeted area toward the elevator, Nancy suddenly froze.

Across the lobby she saw Bill Cooper sitting in the hotel's coffee shop. He was drinking coffee and talking with someone. Nancy did a double take when she realized the other person was Tracy Brandt.

What was going on? Why was Bill Cooper talking to Tracy Brandt, of all people? Nancy and the Hardys had pretty much ruled out Cooper as a suspect, but now she wondered.

Turning to Frank and Joe, she said, "Did you see who I saw?"

"Who?" asked Frank.

"Bill Cooper," said Nancy. She gestured toward the coffee shop. "The woman he's talking with was at Louie's the night we were supposed to meet Pritchitt. Her name's Tracy Brandt."

Frank looked over. "I wonder what they're doing here?" he said in a low voice.

Frowning, Joe said, "I wonder if we're looking at the guy who stole our money?"

"Or the guy who killed Pritchitt? Or the guy who dumped that tray on Frank's head? Or the guy who's the Swallow's contact?" Nancy threw up her hands. "Face it, guys. We have about a zillion questions, but not a single answer so far."

Taking another quick look at Cooper, Frank said, "The waitress just brought them some pie. They'll probably be here for a while. Let's go get Bess and try to make some sense of things. If we don't come up with any brilliant ideas, maybe one of us should follow Cooper. And I wouldn't mind questioning Tracy Brandt, either."

They rode the elevator up to their floor and went into the Hardys' room. Picking up the phone on the desk, Nancy called Bess. She answered on the first ring.

"Where have you been?" she demanded. "It's nearly three o'clock. After what happened to Pritchitt, I was worried!"

"I'm sorry, Bess," said Nancy. "We got tied up. We're in Frank and Joe's room. Come on down and we'll explain everything."

Within two minutes Bess had joined them, taking a seat in front of the room's small desk. "So what happened that you disappeared for practically the whole day?" she asked.

Nancy, Frank, and Joe all started talking at once, giving Bess a rundown on what they had done. Bess furrowed her brow, listening intently.

When Nancy had finished, Bess waited a moment, then turned to Joe. "Wow," she said. "So Louie thinks you and his daughter have a hot romance going?"

The Hardys and Nancy broke into uncontrollable laughter at the same time. "We've been tracking down suspects and fighting fires all day long, and *that's* all you have to say?" Frank sputtered, still laughing.

A look of mock indignation came into Joe's eyes. "Well, *I* appreciate your concern, Bess, even if they don't." He nodded toward his brother and Nancy, who were sitting together on Frank's bed. "I only wish I *was* spending more time with her."

Frank exchanged a worried look with Nancy. Even though Jennifer's one of our suspects? he thought.

Before he could say anything, however, there

was another knock on the door. Beau was waiting outside when Frank opened it.

"Hey there," Beau said, walking into the room. He grinned at Bess. From the bright smile Bess returned, Nancy guessed he had made some progress with her.

"What's going on?" Beau asked, still looking at Bess.

It was Joe who answered. "Not much. How's the law treating you?"

Beau finally tore his gaze away from Bess and looked at the others. "Oh, they're giving me trouble," Beau told them. "They think I stole a guitar. They think I killed a man." He shook his head sadly. "They even think I left you guys that message about meeting me at the duck tank just so you would find the body. Can you believe it?"

Nancy tried to look hopeful. "They just have to consider every possibility," she told him.

"Well, they're considering *me* very carefully," Beau responded. "That's why I came by. I was hoping you might have made some progress on who stole Louie's guitar. Any news?"

"I'm afraid not," said Nancy. "Except that Louie has cooled off on his accusations of you."

"That's good news, anyway," said Beau.

Frank looked questioningly at Beau. "Do you have any ideas about this guitar theft? Any leads we might follow?"

"Well," said Beau, "I did think of one thing. It seems to me that when someone steals something, they usually try to sell it. And around here, the place you'd sell a stolen guitar is a pawnshop. Have you checked out the pawnshops in town?"

"No," Frank replied.

"We don't know the town well," said Joe. "Can you tell us where they are?"

"There's a bunch of them on South Poplar," said Beau. "Head north a few blocks, then hang a right. Maybe a mile out toward midtown there's a little clump of them."

"Don't you think the police have been to the pawnshops already?" Nancy pointed out. "Left-Hand Louie's famous guitar must be pretty recognizable."

"That doesn't mean so much," said Beau. "When you're in Louie's—sure, it's famous. But out in the rest of the world, there's a bunch of guitars that look just like it."

"Won't that make it hard for us to spot it?" asked Joe.

Beau twisted his mouth up. "For a nonexpert, yes," he said. "And I can't go with you, on account of the ducks." He snapped his fingers. "I know," he said suddenly. "You can listen for that rattle sound."

"Rattle?" Nancy echoed.

"That's right," said Beau. "Or more like a buzz. I told you about it before. Happens when you strum a chord."

Nancy nodded, remembering Beau's comment on the noise after playing at Louie's on Monday

129

night. "Do other guitars buzz like that?" she asked Beau.

"Never heard it before in a guitar," Beau answered. "It's kind of odd, really."

"Do you have any idea what might cause it?" Frank asked.

"Maybe a loose part inside the guitar," Beau told him.

"A part *inside* the guitar?" Nancy frowned. "What kind of part?"

"There are these sort of ribs," Beau explained. "For support. One of them could be a little loose."

Nancy looked at the Hardys as an idea struck her. "What if the guitar had something caught in it?" she asked. "Like a piece of paper?"

"That would do it," Beau agreed.

"The information packet!" Frank exclaimed, picking up on Nancy's thought. "Maybe that's where Pritchitt hid the photograph and note."

"There's only one way to find out." Nancy's blue eyes gleamed with excitement.

Joe jumped to his feet. "Hey, that's right," he said. "We looked all over Louie's. But the guitar disappeared before we got to check it. We have to find that guitar."

"I think I'd recognize it," Nancy said. "It has a blue body and a black fingerboard, and there is a blue and red striped strap attached to it."

"That's the one, all right," confirmed Beau. He looked from the Hardys to Nancy, confusion clearly written on his face. But then he broke out into a smile. "I'm not sure what information you're talking about, but good luck. Do you think you can find your way to the pawnshops?"

Joe repeated the directions Beau had given them. Turning to the others, he said, "Ready?"

All five of them left the room, Beau taking an elevator up to the duck tank, and Nancy, Bess, and the Hardys riding down to the lobby.

When they got to the ground floor, Nancy looked toward the coffee shop, but Bill Cooper and Tracy Brandt were no longer there. "If we don't find the guitar and information packet revealing the name of the contact," Nancy said to Frank, "we can find Cooper at his boat later."

Frank and Nancy saw that Joe was waving to someone across the lobby.

"Jennifer," Joe called out.

Nancy looked in the direction he was waving. Sure enough, Jennifer Pardee was walking along the far wall of the lobby. Hearing her name, she looked over at them. When her gaze landed on Joe, Nancy thought Jennifer's expression changed from surprise to exaggerated enthusiasm.

"Hi, Joe!" she called back. She waved but kept walking.

Joe stopped in his tracks. "How do you like that? She's not even coming over to talk to me."

As they watched, Jennifer walked to the bank of telephones and picked one up.

"The phones again," Joe went on, frowning. "What's going on?" For the first time Nancy thought she noticed a glimmer of doubt in his blue eyes.

"Earth to Joe," Frank prodded. "We've got to look for the guitar, remember?"

"Huh—? Oh, right."

The foursome went out to the parking lot and climbed into the convertible, Joe at the wheel. Following Beau's directions, they found the pawnshops just where he said they'd be. There were three of them in a group. Joe parked the car in front of the first one.

The place was set up like a little department store, with areas for different types of items. The musical-instruments section had a long line of guitars hanging on the wall. The gang walked down the row, looking for a guitar like the one Beau had played. They saw three guitars that fit the description, but when they strummed them, none of them had any sort of rattle or buzz.

"Nope," said Frank, handing the last guitar back to the pawnshop owner. "Looks like we'll have to try the next place."

But neither of the other two stores had a guitar that buzzed, either. When Nancy asked the owner of the third store if there were any other pawnshops in town, the man said there were several.

Nancy sighed when they got outside. "Another dead end."

"It doesn't really matter," said Joe. "I mean, can you imagine us checking every guitar in every pawnshop in Memphis? The Swallow would have made his contact and flown the coop long before we'd finished."

Nancy nodded. "You're right, Joe. I say our next step should be to check out Cooper again."

Frank grinned at her. "My sentiments exactly."

"And then we grab some dinner," Joe put in, hopping behind the wheel. "I don't know about you passengers, but the driver is hungry."

"Dinner sounds good to me," Bess agreed as she, Nancy, and Frank climbed into the convertible. "Beau mentioned this place called the Rendezvous. Their barbecued ribs are supposed to be the greatest."

As Joe eased the car forward, a sudden motion in the corner of Nancy's eye caught her attention. Before she even realized why, she found herself yelling, "Everybody down!"

A second later the sound of screeching tires confirmed her instincts. A dark sedan shot into the street beside them. Nancy caught a glimpse of the driver's blond crew cut—and of a rifle barrel sticking out of the passenger window.

Just as she ducked down, four shots rang out.

Chapter

Fourteen

JOE FLINCHED as the four bullets slammed into the side of the red convertible with sickening thuds. The top of the car was down, giving Joe a clear view of the sedan as it roared past.

Joe swiveled quickly around to make sure the others were all right. Then he floored the gas pedal, and the car jerked forward. He spun the wheel left and followed the sedan.

"Don't lose him!" Joe heard his brother call from the backseat. Frank's voice was barely audible over the revving engine and screeching tires.

The sedan made a sudden right onto a side

street. Joe slammed the brake pedal, spun the steering wheel, and skidded into the same street. Glancing down, he saw that the speedometer was pushing fifty. That was about the fastest he could safely go in a populated residential area.

Joe steered the convertible to the right, closely following the sedan as it screeched around another turn. The two cars were about six car lengths apart, but Joe was rapidly closing the distance between them.

The sedan hit another curve. Almost on its bumper now, Joe spun the steering wheel. As the convertible fishtailed, he immediately let up on the gas and began pumping the brake. By the time he regained control of the car, he had lost some distance. He revved the engine even higher.

"We've got trouble, brother!" Frank yelled. "Look."

Ahead of them a dark-haired man was leaning out of the sedan's passenger-side window. He raised the rifle, aiming straight at the convertible.

"Down!" Joe yelled. He hunched as low as he could behind the wheel, while Bess, Nancy, and Frank flattened themselves to the car seats. Four more shots rang out in rapid succession.

Joe felt the car lurch and jerk, and he fought the wheel for control.

"What happened?" Nancy shouted from the backseat.

"They got the front tires," Joe yelled back. The

steering wheel was now bucking and jerking in his hands, and he pumped the brakes until the car bumped to a halt. Far ahead of them the sedan disappeared around a corner.

Instantly Joe leapt out of the car. He stood back to inspect the damage. The two front tires were torn to shreds, the result of blowing out at high speed. In addition, there were four bullet holes in the side panel of the car on Joe's side.

Cracking a weak smile, Joe said, "The guy at the rental place is going to love this."

Bess, who had remained glued to the seat, finally peeked her head up. "Guys, I hate to be the one to break it to you," she complained, "but someone just tried to kill us!"

"It was the same sedan we saw at Louie's," Nancy said. "And the blond guy with the scar was driving."

"They drove away without finishing us off," Frank pointed out. "They may just have been trying to scare us."

Nancy stared down the street in the direction the sedan had gone. "Well, their mission was a success, if that's what they wanted to do," Nancy said. "Next time they'll probably go for blood."

Leaving the others at the car, she found a pay phone and called for a tow truck and a taxi. By the time Frank and Joe had finished explaining to the rental agent what had happened to the convertible, it was after nine o'clock.

"Well, Bill Cooper's boat is already floating somewhere down the Mississippi," Nancy said with a sigh. "We won't be able to talk to him tonight."

Frank gave her a weary smile. "I've had enough action for one day, anyway. Let's eat."

Joe and Bess struck up a chorus of agreement, so Nancy gave in.

The Rendezvous was a large, festive restaurant. And as Bess had promised, the barbecued spareribs were delicious.

"Pass me another napkin, Bess," Joe said, licking a finger. "These ribs are a mess. Worth the effort, though."

"Sure thing, Joe," Bess said.

"Good southern cooking, a fun restaurant, and great friends," she observed, but Nancy managed a poor attempt at a smile.

We may be great friends, she thought, but these days we sure aren't looking like great detectives.

"Okay," said Frank the following morning. He, Joe, Bess, and Nancy were having breakfast in the hotel coffee shop. "Let's go over what we know so far."

Nancy took a deep breath. "Well, we know Klaus's guys are onto us, and that they're giving us pretty strong signals to get off the case."

"Fat chance of that," Joe scoffed. He popped a huge forkful of pancakes drenched with syrup into his mouth.

Next to Joe, Bess was looking thoughtfully down at her plate of scrambled eggs and bacon. "What's the matter, Bess," Frank asked.

Nancy gave her friend a sympathetic look. Bess's boyfriend, Craig, had called them at the hotel to say hello. Nancy knew that Bess was confused about her feelings for him—and for Beau.

"Huh? Oh, nothing," she said. Then, as if forcing herself to think about the case, Bess asked, "What were Klaus's guys doing looking for us at those pawnshops? Do you think they stole the guitar?"

"No way," Joe spoke up. "When Pritchitt called us the day after the guitar had been stolen, he said that he hadn't told Klaus's guys anything. They couldn't have found out about the information packet until the guitar was already missing."

Frank could feel his jaw tensing. Something about the case just wasn't right. "What I want to know," he said slowly, "is how the gunman knew to look for us at the pawnshop? I mean, we didn't tell anyone we were going there. The only person besides us who knew we were going was Beau. And I really doubt he's involved in this."

"Me, too," added Bess adamantly. "He's just not that kind of guy."

"Okay," said Frank. "Let's say it wasn't Beau. There's someone else it could have been."

Frank saw the grim set of his brother's face. "Jennifer," Joe said slowly. "She was in the lobby as we left. I hate to admit it, but she could have alerted someone to follow us."

Nancy could tell it was hard for Joe to admit the possibility. "Don't be so sure," she said, giving him a sympathetic look. "Jennifer may be spying on us, but then again, she may not. If someone was following us from the hotel, they waited a long time before shooting at us."

"Besides," said Joe, "I would have noticed that sedan if it had been following us. It wasn't." He brightened a little. "So maybe Jennifer isn't spying on us."

Nancy frowned. "You may be right. But how did Klaus's guys know where to find us? It doesn't make sense."

Frank's face took on a look of intense concentration for a moment. "Maybe it does make sense. If you think about it, there are a lot of things Klaus knows about our investigation."

The others stopped eating and looked at him. "What do you mean?" asked Nancy.

"Look at it this way," said Frank. "Assume that Klaus and his agents don't know who the Swallow's contact is. They killed Pritchitt before he could tell them. So here they are in the same position we're in—they're trying to figure out who the Swallow's contact is."

"Right," said Joe. "So?"

"Okay," said Frank. "Now, when we went out to Pritchitt's, did it look like anyone had searched the place before us?"

"No," said Nancy. "Nothing seemed to have been disturbed."

"But that's where we figured out that the contact was one of Pritchitt's poker buddies. The question is, how did Klaus's guys figure that out?"

"Maybe they didn't," Bess piped in.

"But they did," Nancy reminded her. "Klaus's operatives questioned Jack Arvis—"

"Who at one point was our primary suspect!" Joe finished. "But how could Klaus know that?"

Nancy took a sip of juice, thinking fast. "You're right," she said. "We were talking about Arvis before we went, but only among ourselves."

"Exactly," Frank said, then added, "In our hotel room."

"Are you thinking what I'm thinking?" Nancy asked him.

The gleam in Frank's eyes told her the answer to her question. "Let's pay the check," she said, rising to her feet and waving to the waitress. They all put some money on the table and left the restaurant, heading for the elevators. On the third floor Nancy paused outside the Hardys' room.

"Remember," she said. "You were robbed."

"How can we forget?" Joe replied.

"What I mean is, someone broke into your room," Nancy continued. "Your guest could have invited himself back." She put her finger to her lips, then signaled Joe to open the door. He did, and they followed him inside.

Nancy looked around for a moment, then walked to the desk. She picked up the phone and examined it. Nothing. She opened a couple of the drawers. Nothing there, either. Then she tilted the lamp down and looked inside its shade.

Suppressing an urge to cry out, she motioned excitedly for the others to come look. A tiny microphone was inside the shade, stuck near the metal bracket that held it to the lamp. The device was nearly invisible.

They'd been bugged!

Chapter

Fifteen

BESS GAPED as she stared at the microphone. She began to say something, but Nancy held a finger up to silence her.

Quietly Nancy led the rest of the gang out into the hall and closed the door.

"Wow!" Bess exclaimed. "That was a great hunch, Frank."

Nancy looked admiringly at Frank and said, "She's right. Way to go. Now, at least, we won't feed Klaus any more information."

"But they've heard so much already," Frank said.

"Are you going to get rid of it?" Bess asked.

"It might be better if Klaus and his crew didn't know we're onto them," Frank explained. "Also, I'm thinking maybe we can use the bug to send false information. The bug could actually help our case."

"Beating the thugs with their own bugs," Joe quipped, with a grin.

Bess rolled her eyes at Joe.

"At least it explains all those coincidences," Nancy said. "Let's go down to the lobby to talk things over. You never know—they may have bugged Bess's and my room as well."

Frank nodded. "The lobby's so wide open, it would be impossible to bug. And it'll be easy for us to spot anyone listening in on us."

"Besides," Bess added with a grin, "I just love those sofas and chairs. They're so luxurious."

Down in the lobby the foursome settled into a fairly secluded corner.

"Well, gang," said Joe. "If we want to think of some way to use this bug, we'd better do it fast. It's Thursday, and the meeting is set for midnight tonight."

"That's a problem," Frank stated, frowning. "Using a bug this way is usually a waiting game. You can't know for sure when someone is listening in."

"Couldn't you set a trap for Klaus and his men?" asked Bess. "You could say you're going to be somewhere at a specific time, then wait for them there."

Joe shook his head. "No good. What if they don't get the message?" he asked. "Then we've lost valuable time. We've only got about fourteen hours to find the Swallow's contact."

"Yeah," said Frank. "And at this point so do Klaus's goons. They're not going to waste any more time tracking us down. They know everything we've figured out by now. They're probably looking all over for that stolen guitar."

"And that's what we should be doing," said Nancy, wondering where they could start.

As her eyes wandered aimlessly around the lobby, she noticed Bill Cooper sitting in an armchair across the room. He was reading a newspaper, and a cup of coffee sat on the table in front of him.

"Look," Nancy said to the others. "There's Bill Cooper. This is the second time he's been here in two days."

Joe shrugged. "Well, he's here, not at the Gulf of Mexico. And he's not exactly acting suspicious."

"Maybe he's catching a plane later today," Bess suggested.

"Good morning, everyone!" Beau's bright, melodic voice rang out from across the lobby as he strode up to the gang.

Bess turned and smiled at him. "Hi!" she said. But then she seemed to think that was too encouraging. She slumped back in her chair and stared down at her hands. When Beau asked how she was, Bess just mumbled, "Fine," without looking at him.

A moment later she stood up and said, "I have to check and see if I've gotten any messages." She moved quickly away.

Nancy knew Bess had come up with an excuse to get away from Beau. Seeing the hurt and confusion on Beau's face, Nancy had to admit she sympathized with him. Beau was such a warm, open guy, and he really liked Bess. Nancy was pretty sure Bess was getting to like him more and more, too. Talking to Craig on the phone must have made her feel guilty about Beau. Nancy sighed. If avoiding Beau meant making herself miserable, Nancy didn't see what good that did Bess.

"Bess doesn't seem to be interested in me," Beau said, staring disconsolately after her.

Nancy was about to respond when suddenly a voice from behind her did instead. "Don't ever say that about yourself, Beau."

It was Bill Cooper. He stood behind Nancy, smiling sympathetically. "You'd be a great catch for any girl," he went on, placing a hand on Beau's shoulder. "And you're making a big effort to impress the young lady. That's what she's going to notice."

"Oh, she noticed all right, Captain Billy," Beau said. "You saw her go running away."

Curious, Nancy asked, "You know each other?"

Cooper nodded. "Sure. I come here to eat sometimes when I'm too lazy to cook for myself. Beau is an easy kind of guy to strike up a friendship with."

Then maybe it was simply coincidence that had brought Cooper here two days in a row, Nancy thought.

The captain turned back to Beau. "Sometimes it takes a while for things to take hold," he said. "Give it a chance. Love can be difficult and almost seem impossible at times. But in the end it's always worth it."

Beau looked intently at Cooper. "How do you know so much about all this, Billy?" he asked. "I've never seen you with a girlfriend."

"Well, I have one," Cooper said with a smile. "She's from out of town."

"Madeline," Nancy said, recalling the photograph aboard Cooper's riverboat.

Cooper seemed surprised that Nancy remembered. "That's right," he confirmed after a moment. "Madeline Swift. Nancy's seen her picture," he explained to the others.

Nancy nodded to Beau. "And she's beautiful," she assured him.

"Don't talk to me about beautiful women," Beau said morosely. "Bess is really pretty. Maybe I'm just not her type."

"That's the wrong attitude," Cooper said. "You need to think positively. That's how you'll win Bess over."

"Hmph," Beau grunted. But he seemed to consider what Cooper was saying.

Joe leaned forward and slapped Beau on the arm. "That's right," he said encouragingly. "A positive attitude is very attractive to women. It works for me."

Nancy rolled her eyes, but she couldn't help smiling. Soon they were all laughing.

"Thanks for the advice," Beau told them. "I'm going to try to keep that in mind." Checking his watch, he added, "It's just about time for the ducks, so I've got to get going."

Cooper smiled and called after Beau, "Chin up, son." With that, he waved his folded newspaper and started walking away.

"Mr. Cooper," Nancy called after him. She didn't want to miss her chance to question him.

He turned. "Hmm?"

Giving him a bright smile, Nancy said, "Tonight's the night for the riverboat ride."

"I'm looking forward to seeing you there," he said with a nod.

"See you later," Nancy said. She had been hoping that Cooper would show some sign of being the Swallow's contact. Nancy was disappointed. It still didn't look as though he'd be going to the Gulf of Mexico tonight.

"Uh-oh," Frank said under his breath to Nancy. "Here comes another love problem."

"What did you say?" Joe asked, having overheard his brother.

Frank pointed across the lobby. Jennifer Pardee had just walked in. Joe broke into a grin and waved. For a moment it seemed as if Jennifer had seen them, but then she turned away. Keeping her eyes averted, she walked along the far wall, toward the telephones.

"I know she saw me," Joe said, frowning. "What's going on?"

"She's back to the phones," Nancy said suspiciously. "Doesn't look good, Joe."

Joe looked puzzled but only for a moment. Then his expression changed to determination, and he jumped to his feet. "I'm going to clear this up right now," he said.

"Joe, take it easy," Frank cautioned, but Joe stormed off across the lobby. Nancy and Frank chased after him.

When they reached Jennifer, she was holding a house phone. She turned just in time to see Joe's approach. With a slight gasp, she lowered the phone.

Joe put his finger on the cradle, breaking the phone connection. "All right," he demanded. "You've got some explaining to do."

Chapter

Sixteen

FRANK COULD SEE that Joe's outburst had frightened Jennifer. "W-what are you talking about?" she stammered, shrinking back.

"Hey, Joe—" Frank put a restraining hand on his brother's arm.

Joe shook it off. "Every time we see her in this lobby, she takes one look at us and goes to the telephone."

The look Jennifer gave Joe was filled with guilt. Then she looked down in silence. She seemed to be hiding beneath her long brown hair.

"Who do you talk to?" Joe asked, putting his hands on his hips. "And what are you telling them? Are you tipping off the Swallow about our movements?"

Frank cringed. He didn't think it was a good idea for Joe to divulge any information about their case.

"I don't know what you're talking about," Jennifer said in confusion. "Who's the Swallow?"

Before Frank could stop his brother from saying anything more, Joe blurted out, "Don't play dumb. You've been using me, haven't you?"

Jennifer sank her face in her hands. "Yes," she mumbled. "I *have* been using you. I feel terrible." Her shoulders shook with silent tears.

Frank stared in surprise. Jennifer was cracking awfully easily for someone who was supposed to be involved in serious spy business.

"*You* feel terrible?" Joe burst out. "You nearly got us killed!"

"Let her explain, Joe," Nancy cut in.

Jennifer wiped her eyes. "I don't have a clue about who or what the Swallow is. And I don't know what you mean about getting you killed. What I *do* know"—she hesitated, stumbling over the words—"is that I'm in love. You're nice, Joe. But I'm already in love with someone else."

Frank saw his brother's jaw drop in surprise.

"I'm in love with Tad Baker," Jennifer admitted. "He works here at the hotel. But my father won't let me see him."

"Why not?" Nancy asked. Frank saw that

Nancy seemed as off-balance as Joe. How did this fit in with their case—or did it at all?

"Dad's got this hang-up," Jennifer explained, embarrassed. "I can't go out with hotel workers. He says it's as bad as dating a restaurant man."

Frank stared. "But *he's* a restaurant man."

Jennifer nodded. "That's what makes it so weird. I guess he knows what it's like to work long hours in a business that can be unpredictable. He wants me to find somebody stable."

"So where do I fit in?" Joe was still baffled. Frank could understand why.

"You're smart, you're cute, and you don't work in a restaurant," Jennifer told him. "When I found out you were staying at the hotel, I knew it would give me a good excuse to come here." She looked at him with teary eyes. "That's why I introduced you to my dad that first night I met you. Now I tell him I'm going out with you, and he doesn't ask any questions."

"And I thought you found me irresistible," Joe said with humor in his eyes. Frank noticed Joe had perked up at being called smart and cute.

Nancy had kept quiet during most of the exchange with Jennifer, but now she stepped forward. Something was bothering her about Jennifer's story. "You still haven't explained why you're always talking on the phone here," she said. "Why not just go to the front desk?"

"Tad's nervous about keeping his job," Jennifer said sheepishly. "His boss doesn't like him goofing off during his shift. So when I show up at the hotel, I call Tad on the house phone. That way his boss can't tell who he's talking to. Sometimes Tad makes an excuse to disappear for a while, and the two of us have time together. It wasn't nice to do," she admitted, "but it was the only way I had to see him. I'm really sorry."

Joe sighed. "That's okay."

Nancy was glad to see Joe had taken Jennifer's rejection well. Smiling, Nancy thought to herself, If I know Joe Hardy, he'll have no trouble finding other dates.

"I feel terrible about it," Jennifer added. "You just have to understand how hard it is living with my father."

Wheels raced in Nancy's mind. Maybe Jennifer could give them information about Louie. After all, they hadn't been able to cross him off the list of suspects yet. With a sympathetic smile Nancy said casually, "Having a stubborn parent can be hard in all sorts of ways, not just dating."

Jennifer shrugged. "A dad's a dad, I guess."

"How about working for him in the restaurant?" Nancy asked, steering the conversation in Louie's direction.

"Well, he's *always* around, and he likes to have his own way." Jennifer sighed. "But he's not a bad guy deep down."

Nancy hesitated, hoping her next question wouldn't seem so obvious. "Still, I bet it's a break for everyone at the restaurant when he goes out of town—like tonight."

Jennifer gave her a puzzled look. "Out of town? My father will be at the restaurant tonight, like he always is. Why would he leave town?"

"Oh," said Nancy, searching for an answer.

"What's going on here?"

Nancy was never so glad to see Tad Baker—even if his face had a look of suspicion in it.

"When your call was cut off, I got worried," Tad told Jennifer. "But there'll be trouble if my boss sees me out here."

"No sweat," said Joe. "We were just leaving."

"Right," Nancy said as she followed Joe and Frank back to the sofa and chairs, where they'd been before spotting Jennifer. Bess had returned and was sitting in a chair waiting for them.

"Well," said Nancy, after telling Bess what she had missed, "it doesn't look like Louie's going out of town tonight. And neither is Bill Cooper. That leaves us pretty much nowhere."

"Unless we find that guitar," Joe said.

Frank shook his head. "We can't waste any more time on that," he said.

"There's one other possible lead." Nancy paused, trying to organize her thoughts. "When we saw Cooper yesterday, he was talking to a woman named Tracy Brandt." She reminded her friends that she'd seen Tracy Brandt at Louie's their first night in Memphis and twice more, at the hotel.

"It could be just a coincidence," Nancy said, "but at this point, it's all we've got."

"Maybe one of us should stay here at the hotel to see if she comes back," Joe suggested.

"I had something a bit more practical in mind," Nancy replied. "She told me she was setting up a stereo store at the Pyramid. Why don't we go there and see if we can talk to her?"

Frank nodded. "It's better than sitting around, hoping for this case to solve itself." Bess and Joe nodded in agreement.

"Okay," Joe said. "But given our luck with cars, this time I insist we take a taxi."

After finding the main entrance, the four teenagers stood at the ground floor of the Pyramid, looking at a map of the complex.

"Funny," Nancy mused. "There's no music store listed—although there does seem to be some sort of music hall here."

"Maybe it's not listed because it hasn't opened yet," Frank suggested. "Come on. There must be an office where we can ask."

After a brief search they found the management office, a modern-looking room with two high-tech chrome-and-glass desks in it. A blueprint of the Pyramid hung on the wall. Next to it a calendar indicated upcoming sports and music events being held at the complex.

Nancy looked up as a woman in slacks, a

blazer, and wire-framed glasses entered from a back room. "Can I help you?" the woman asked.

"Yes," replied Nancy. "I have some questions about a business here at the Pyramid."

"Yes?" The woman raised her eyebrows.

"I've heard there's going to be an audio store here," Nancy went on. "Can you tell us where it is, and if we might be able to visit it?"

Behind Nancy, Joe piped up, "Yes, we represent a Japanese audio firm, and we're interested in supplying the new store."

"An audio store?" The woman shook her head. "I'm afraid we have a misunderstanding here. The Great American Pyramid is *not* a shopping mall," she said. "It's an entertainment complex. We have a sports arena, two museums, and a restaurant. There are no retail outlets."

Nancy looked at the woman in confusion. "But I spoke to a woman named Tracy Brandt who said she was setting up an audio store. Are you sure it isn't in the works?"

"Quite sure," the woman told her. "The only money-making venture of that sort is the Rock Spot, our restaurant. Money-losing, I should say. We certainly don't need any more risks like that."

"The Rock Spot isn't doing well?" Frank asked.

The woman hesitated, then leaned forward. "The Rock Spot is doing terribly," she confided.

"And it's because of the owner, Jeff Eliot. The management company is regretting their decision to allow him to open the restaurant. They've been putting pressure on Mr. Eliot to try to get him to sell out to them."

"Why doesn't he?" Frank asked.

"Oh, he will," said the woman, with a knowing nod. "When the Rock Spot fails. He's promised the management company he'll have people lined up outside the door by the end of next month." She dismissed this idea with a wave of her hand. "I'll believe that when I see it."

Joe spoke up from behind Nancy. "So there's not going to be any sort of audio store?" he asked. Nancy could tell he was eager to get back on the case.

"No," said the woman. "Nor any other kind of store. This Tracy Brandt was giving you a story."

"I see," said Nancy. "Thank you for your time." She led the others out the door.

As soon as they were outside the Pyramid, Nancy turned to the Hardys and Bess. "Tracy Brandt was lying to me," she announced grimly.

Bess's blue eyes were filled with confusion. "But why would she lie about something like that?"

"Because she doesn't want us to know why she's really in town. I bet anything she's tied to this case somehow—either she's the Swallow's contact, or she's working for Klaus."

Just then a car pulled up to the curb, and Jeff

Eliot jumped out. He wore his usual white suit and panama hat. His cane swung jauntily as he walked into the Rock Spot. He didn't seem to notice the teenagers.

"Something's wrong." Frank stared after him.

"What are you talking about?" Nancy asked.

"There was something off about Eliot," Frank said. Closing his eyes, he muttered, "The white suit, the hat, the cane," as if ticking off Jeff Eliot's features in his mind. Suddenly his eyes popped open. "The cane!" he shouted.

Joe rolled his eyes. "Will you stop talking Swahili and make some sense?" he said impatiently.

Frank ignored his brother. "Remember that metal cylinder we found by the fire in Louie's Dumpster? It was made of brass."

Nancy's face lit with understanding. "Like the tip of that cane Jeff Eliot always carries around," she finished. "Is that what you saw?"

Frank nodded. "When Jeff was waving his cane around just now, it was missing its brass tip. Jeff Eliot set the fire at Louie's!"

Chapter

Seventeen

Y**OU'RE RIGHT, FRANK,**" Joe said. "It makes perfect sense. Eliot needs to make his restaurant a hit. The most popular place in town is Left-Hand Louie's. First Eliot tries to copy Louie's, but that doesn't work. Nobody wants a cheap imitation."

"So he decides to get rid of his main competition," Bess added. "He tries to burn Louie's down."

Joe grinned at her. "You got it!"

Nancy felt a sudden rush of excitement. "Wait a minute, guys. He did something else first." The others looked at her expectantly. "First, he stole

Louie's guitar. It had to be Jeff Eliot. That guitar draws lots of people to Louie's."

Frank and Joe looked at each other and exclaimed at the same time, "Pritchitt's information!"

"Jeff Eliot's had it all this time," Frank said, shaking his head in amazement. "But where do you think he's keeping the guitar?"

A slow smile appeared on Nancy's face. "Remember when we talked to Spence Burbank at the Rock Spot?" she asked after a short silence. "One of the things he said was that the Rock Spot was a great place to work because Jeff Eliot was such a good boss. He said Eliot always insisted on getting things from the supply closet himself. He wouldn't let Spence go in there."

"You think he's hiding the guitar in the supply closet?" Joe asked.

"I think it's a good bet," Nancy responded.

Now Joe grinned. "Well, let's sneak in and find that guitar."

"It's not going to be that simple," Frank cautioned. "If Eliot won't let his own waiter in the supply closet, he's definitely not going to let us in there. And I doubt we could divert him, either. As soon as he sees any of us, he'd just kick us out. I mean, we're not exactly on good terms with him now."

Joe cringed, remembering the insults he'd hurled at Jeff Eliot the day before. "He deserved it, but you're right. We'll have to wait until the Rock Spot closes and sneak in."

"Remember, the meeting between the Swallow and his contact is supposed to be at midnight on the Gulf of Mexico," Nancy pointed out. "How will we get the information from the guitar in time to follow the contact down there? For all we know, the contact has already left town."

Joe asked, "Do you have any better ideas?"

"We can look for Tracy Brandt," Nancy suggested. "Question her to see if she knows something about the case."

"We can split up," Joe suggested. "I'll go after the guitar and you three go after Tracy Brandt."

"Sounds like a good plan," Frank said after a moment. "Let's face it. We're not heading down to the gulf anytime soon—at least, not without pinpointing a rendezvous spot."

"Let's find out when the Rock Spot closes," said Joe. He started toward the restaurant, but Nancy held him back.

"I'll go," she told him. "I think it would be better if you keep clear of Jeff Eliot."

To Nancy's relief, Eliot wasn't in sight when she entered the Rock Spot. Spence stood by the cash register.

He recognized Nancy and smiled. "Eating by yourself?" he asked. "Where are your friends?"

Without answering Spence's second question, Nancy said, "I'm not eating right now."

"You come here a lot, but you never seem to

eat. What's going on?" Spence seemed more amused than annoyed.

"We plan to eat here," Nancy lied, "but we want to eat dinner. I'm here to find out how late you're open tonight."

"We're supposed to be open until eleven," Spence said. "But the last few nights have been real slow. Mr. Eliot lets us go and closes the restaurant early." From his contented smile Nancy could tell it was an arrangement Spence liked.

"About what time?" she asked him.

"Nine-thirty or so," Spence replied. "Guess the boss figures if no one shows up by then, it's a lost cause." He laughed nervously, as if he weren't sure an employee should be laughing at his boss's problems.

"So around eight would be good?" Nancy asked.

Spence nodded. "That sounds about right."

"Okay," said Nancy. She had been glancing around, trying to figure out how Joe could sneak in later. "Say, is there a bathroom around here?" she asked suddenly.

"Sure," said Spence, pointing behind him. "It's back that way."

Five minutes later she rejoined the Hardys and Bess outside. "The bathroom has a window," she told them, "and I left it unlocked for you, Joe. To make sure it stays that way, I removed the latch." Grinning, she held up the small metal fitting.

Joe laughed. "One less problem," he said.

"Good going," Frank told her, clapping Nancy on the shoulder.

Joe's expression grew serious. "I'm going to come down here around nine-thirty," said Joe. "Once the place goes dark I'll wait about fifteen minutes to be safe. Then I'll go through the window and have a look around."

"Be careful," Bess warned, a worried expression in her blue eyes. "This sounds a little dangerous to me."

Joe smiled appreciatively at her. "As soon as I've checked the storeroom," he went on, "I'll call the Peabody's front desk and leave a message for you. 'Dinner was great,' means I found the guitar. 'Dinner was lousy,' means I haven't. Then I'll head straight back to the hotel. So you can arrange to meet me in the lobby. That is, unless you've found Tracy Brandt and gotten something out of her."

"In that case we'll leave a message, telling you where to meet us," Nancy finished.

"Well, now that we know what we're doing tonight, let's talk about what we'll do today," Bess spoke up.

"Like what?" asked Joe.

"There is more to life than mysteries, you know," Bess replied. "And there's more to Memphis. For instance, there's Graceland—"

Bess tried to look stern, but it was hard to do when the other teenagers dissolved into laughter.

"It's a promise," Nancy said. "We'll take you to Graceland."

"Bess, that's the fifth outfit you've tried on," Nancy said, looking at the growing pile of skirts and dresses on Bess's bed. "We were supposed to meet Frank and Joe in the coffee shop ten minutes ago."

"Does this look all right?" Bess asked, glancing nervously at her white blouse and ankle-length blue skirt. "I mean, it's not too, um—romantic —is it?"

That was a change, Nancy thought. Often Bess tried to dress in a romantic style.

"You always look great no matter what you have on. Anyway, you could be wearing a paper bag, and Beau would still think you were gorgeous."

Bess's face lit up. "He would? I mean—not that I want him to," she amended hastily. "I have Craig, after all."

Nancy took a deep breath. "You know," she said, "we've been so busy with the case that we really haven't had much time to talk about the really important things"—her blue eyes gleamed —"like boys."

Flopping down on her bed, Bess moaned and said, "What am I going to do? I mean, I think Craig is great. But when I see Beau, he's so sweet, and, well, I want to spend time with him, too."

"Some problem," Nancy said, grinning. "Maybe you should just enjoy yourself. It's not a crime, you know."

Bess shot her a teasing smile. "Nancy Drew! What would Ned say if he heard you talking that way?"

"We're not talking about me," she pointed out with a grin.

When she and Bess got to the coffee shop, Nancy saw that the Hardys weren't alone. Beau sat with them at the table.

"Talk about good timing," she whispered to Bess. "Go ahead and knock his socks off!"

She noticed that this time Bess's hello was just as sunny and smiling as Beau's.

"We were just about to tell Beau the good news," Joe told the girls.

"What's that?" Bess and Beau asked at once. Then they grinned at each other and laughed.

"I think we've figured out who stole Louie's guitar," Joe said.

Beau's green eyes widened. "No fooling?" he said. "Wow, that's great! Who is it?"

"Do you know Jeff Eliot?" Joe asked. "He owns the Rock Spot, that restaurant in the Great American Pyramid."

Beau thought for a moment, then nodded. "Yeah," he said. "He's the guy who came up to me at Louie's and told me he wanted me to play at his restaurant."

"He's the one," said Nancy.

"His restaurant is in trouble," Frank explained. "And Left-Hand Louie's is his main competition. We think he's been trying to sabotage Louie's, first by stealing the guitar, then by trying to burn the restaurant down." Frank told Beau about finding the brass tip of Eliot's cane near where the fire had been set.

"We're going to check into it further tonight," Joe added. "So you should be cleared soon."

Beau snapped his fingers. "Hey! I'll bet Eliot's the one who called me out to Sun Studios. Now that I think of it, I gave him my phone number that afternoon. I thought there was something familiar about the voice of the guy who called about recording. It must have been Jeff Eliot, trying to frame me. He didn't use his real name when he identified himself."

"That's right," said Nancy, looking at the Hardys. "We forgot about that phone call. But it fits right in with our theory."

With a grin at Beau Frank added, "It even strengthens the case against him."

Beau let out a loud whoop. "Great!" he shouted. "I'll be off the hook." His green eyes sparkled down at Bess. "This is even more cause for celebration. I'm going to take you out for lunch. I won't take no for an answer."

Bess returned his look with a flirtatious smile. "On one condition," she told him. "After lunch I want to go to Graceland."

Beau's face broke into a wide grin. "You've got

it." He made an exaggerated bow toward Nancy and the Hardys. "Will you excuse us?" he asked with mock gallantry.

"Well, actually, I had my heart set on going to Graceland with Bess," Joe replied.

"Struck out again, bro," Frank pointed out.

They all laughed as Beau held his arm for Bess, playing the perfect southern gentleman as he escorted her to the hotel entrance. She placed a hand in the crook of his arm, her cheeks blushing a bright pink.

"I thought we'd start with lunch at the Rendezvous. And then—" His voice cut off as the door closed behind them.

"What a character," said Frank.

Still chuckling, Nancy took a step toward the door, watching Bess and Beau. They crossed the street and entered the alley that led to the Rendezvous.

Suddenly Nancy froze. Entering the alley behind Beau and Bess were two men. One of them was the blond man with the scar on his lip. The other one was the dark-haired man who had shot at them from the sedan.

"Frank! Joe!" she called frantically. "It's Klaus's men. They're after Bess and Beau—and they've got guns!"

Chapter

Eighteen

NANCY'S HEART LEAPT into her mouth. This couldn't be happening.

Joe sprinted past her and burst through the hotel door. Frank and Nancy were right behind him. As her feet hit the sidewalk, Nancy saw the dark-haired man reach her friends. Jumping Beau from behind, he slammed him against the wall. The blond man with the crew cut grabbed Bess.

"Hold it!" Nancy shouted, running into the street.

Suddenly a familiar dark sedan skidded to a halt in front of the alley. Nancy gasped when she saw who was at the wheel—Tracy Brandt! The woman must be working for Klaus.

Tracy Brandt leaned out the window to level a gun at Nancy. "Hold it right there," she snapped.

Nancy did as ordered. "Leave them alone!" she shouted. "They have nothing to do with you."

"Split up, Joe!" Nancy heard Frank yell. "She can't cover both of us."

Nancy stood helpless as the brothers darted in opposite directions, Frank in front of the sedan, Joe behind.

"Stop," Tracy Brandt commanded. "Or I'll shoot your friend Miss Drew." The gun on Nancy didn't waver.

Frank and Joe froze.

Nancy felt a chill invade her entire body. The blond operative had his arm around Bess now, his gun pointed at her head. Bess looked to be frozen with fear, her eyes widened in shock.

"Hurry up!" Tracy Brandt spat. "It's broad daylight. We have to get out of here."

The blond thug pushed Bess forward, keeping his pistol close to her temple. Then he pushed Bess into the car. "Come on," he called to the other operative.

The dark-haired agent, who had been holding Beau's arm twisted behind him at a painful angle, threw him to the ground. Then the spy hopped in the back of the sedan, and it sped away with screeching tires.

Nancy ran a few steps after the car, but gave up when it careened around a corner. She got a last glimpse of Bess's panic-stricken face in the rear window as the sedan disappeared. A sick feeling rose in Nancy like a huge wave. She'd have fallen to the ground if Frank hadn't caught her.

"We'll find her," he whispered consolingly.

But Nancy knew Frank had no idea if they would. Klaus's operatives had already killed one person. Who knew what they had in store for Bess?

Beau came up to them, rubbing his wrenched arm. His face was white with shock. He seemed unhurt, except for a scraped knee that could be seen through the rip in his pants. "What's going on?" he demanded hoarsely. "What are they doing with Bess?"

Nancy could hardly think straight. She was grateful for Frank's arm around her.

"She's been kidnapped," Frank said. "That means they think we're too close to solving this thing—or maybe they still don't know any more than we do and want an edge. Face it, if they knew who the contact was, they'd just **go** after him instead of wasting time with Bess."

Trying to pull herself together, Nancy said grimly, "We've got to do something to get Bess back." She took a deep breath. "We'll call the police," she said. "Maybe they can find that sedan. We also need to see if we can find out where Tracy Brandt is staying." Her mind raced, trying to come up with every possible way of rescuing Bess.

"You're right," Joe agreed. "But I think we'd better start our own rescue mission, too. We've got to find Bess and head off Klaus before midnight tonight."

"What can I do to help?" Beau asked. The worried look in his green eyes pulled at Nancy's heart.

"You hit the local hotels and see if one of them has a woman named Tracy Brandt listed in its register," Joe told him. "If there's no Tracy Brandt, describe her and see if she's checked in under another name."

"I didn't really get a look at her," Beau admitted. "That gorilla was busy pushing my face into a wall. But I sure remember what *he* looked like."

"Well, he's staying somewhere, too," said Nancy. "See if you can track him down." She described Tracy Brandt to Beau, and he went off to see what he could find.

Frank and Joe headed back inside the hotel lobby with Nancy, who called the police from one of the pay phones. She didn't think they'd believe any story about the Swallow and Klaus, so she just reported that Bess had been abducted and that she didn't know who had done it.

"Okay," Nancy said after hanging up the phone. "Let's start searching." She looked urgently from Frank to Joe. "They could be anywhere. Where do we begin?"

Frank's face took on a thoughtful expression. "Well," he said, "we could rent another car and search for that dark sedan."

"Rent a car?" Joe groaned. "Isn't there another way?"

Nancy couldn't help smiling. "We don't have to go to the same rental agency," she suggested.

"Yes, we do," Joe said miserably. "It's the only one downtown. The rest are all out at the airport."

"Not *you* again!"

Frank ignored the rental agent's horrified look. "I need to rent a car," he said.

"That's a laugh." The agent scowled. "Your brother's already destroyed two. What makes you think I'm going to let you have another one?"

"I'm a much safer driver than my brother." Frank was growing impatient, but he managed to keep a smile on his face. "I need that car—and I only get dangerous when people don't help when I need things desperately."

"The insurance," the agent began.

"There won't be another accident," Frank told him confidently. "It's a matter of life and death."

The agent seemed to soften a little, but Frank could tell he hadn't given in yet. "I can't give you another one of those Jerry Lee Lewis specials. How about something else?"

"Please," Frank said.

The rental agent finally gave in. "But your brother better not do any driving," he warned.

Ten minutes later Frank, Joe, and Nancy were squeezed into a silver compact car. Sitting in back, Joe had to stretch his legs out sideways on the seat, because his bent knees wouldn't fit behind the front seat. Nancy and Frank, in front, didn't have the luxury of spreading out. Nancy's left knee kept knocking into Frank's right as they drove.

"I guess this is better than nothing," Nancy said, trying to be optimistic.

"I feel like a pretzel," said Joe.

"That's probably better than how Bess feels right now," Nancy said.

"You're right," Joe said. "We've got to find her."

They drove through the main downtown area, looking for the sedan.

"It just doesn't make sense that the kidnappers would take Bess to somewhere around here," said Nancy, scanning the sidewalks as Frank maneuvered the compact through the heavy downtown traffic. "Almost everything down here is office buildings. A stranger from out of town probably wouldn't risk attracting attention by dragging a hostage into one of these buildings."

"What about Pritchitt's house?" Joe asked from the backseat. "Maybe Klaus's guys are using the place as a kind of headquarters."

Turning the car north, Frank drove to the run-down house, but it was empty and undisturbed.

"Let's try south," Nancy suggested.

She knew from her map that the area south of downtown was the old cotton district, where people bought and sold cotton during the old plantation days, to ship up and down the Mississippi River. Heading south, she and the Hardys saw dozens of large, elegant buildings empty and deserted. Others had been converted into apartments and condominiums.

Frank turned a corner and came across a run-down old hotel. Next to it was a pool hall. "I don't know," Frank said doubtfully. "That place looks pretty shabby, even for those goons."

"There's no sedan, either," Joe pointed out.

"And no Bess," Nancy added. She bit back the feeling of helplessness and kept her eyes trained carefully on their surroundings.

The road dipped down under some railroad tracks. As they passed beneath them, Nancy looked to her left.

"Frank!" she shouted. "Stop the car!"

Frank jammed on the brakes, and Nancy felt herself jerk against the safety harness. "What is it?" he asked.

"Look!" cried Nancy, pointing.

The train tracks passed over the road on a trestle with a thick stone base on either side.

Weeds and bushes grew up around the stone. And sitting right in the middle of the scrubby growth was a red pickup truck.

"That's Hank Pritchitt's truck!" Frank exclaimed, pulling the car over.

Nancy and the Hardys climbed out of the car and ran over to the truck.

"It's definitely the one we saw driving away from Louie's that night," Joe said excitedly.

"What do you think it's doing here?" Frank asked, glancing around the deserted, run-down area. "Do you think Klaus's base of operations is nearby? Or did his men just dump the truck here to get rid of it?"

Nancy followed his gaze but didn't see anything suspicious. "I'd be willing to bet a top spy like Klaus wouldn't dump evidence anywhere near where he's staying." Nodding toward the truck, she added, "But at least this truck is evidence of some kind. I'll bet it's crawling with fingerprints."

"That's right," said Joe. He seemed unable to stand still and kept shifting from one foot to the other. "But since they're from another country, they don't have to worry about their prints being on file here. And they probably plan to leave the country tomorrow."

"But if we catch them," Nancy said, "the prints on this truck could be used to put them behind bars. They'd be solid evidence."

"If we catch them," Frank repeated. "Which we're not doing too well at the moment."

Nancy sighed in frustration. "We're still not any closer to finding Bess. Let's go back to the hotel and report this truck to the police. They should get a team working on it right away."

"Maybe Beau found out where Tracy Brandt is staying," Frank said.

"The police haven't found Bess yet," Nancy said dejectedly.

She, Frank, and Joe were back in the lobby of the Peabody. Nancy had just used the pay phone to call the police and tell them about the pickup truck. The officer she spoke to told her he'd leave a message at the hotel if Bess was found.

"Hey, did you guys even hear me?" Nancy asked.

The Hardys hadn't even looked up. They were hunched over a piece of paper. Then Nancy noticed how pale Frank's face had gotten.

"Frank, what is it?" she demanded.

He handed the sheet to Nancy. It said, "We have your friend. We won't hesitate to kill her. Forget about the Swallow. She's ours."

Chapter

Nineteen

NANCY GASPED. "Poor Bess!"

Frank's jaw tensed as he read the note again. "I don't think they're bluffing."

"Those creeps," Joe muttered angrily.

But Frank barely heard his brother. His eyes had lingered on a word at the bottom of the note. "Hey," he said suddenly, "the Swallow is a woman!"

"A woman?" Nancy began thinking furiously. "This changes everything," she said.

Frank wasn't sure how, but he was glad they had something new to go on.

"You're not kidding!" Joe exclaimed.

"We were looking for a male agent before," Nancy began. "Arvis's brother, for example. But now that we know the Swallow's a woman . . ." She paused for a moment. "I think Bill Cooper is a strong candidate to be her contact."

"How do you figure?" Joe asked.

"When Bess and I were on the *River Queen*, we saw a picture of Cooper's girlfriend—her name is Madeline." Nancy frowned, trying to remember the scene exactly. "He told us that he hasn't seen her for a while, but he'd be seeing her soon. And who's supposed to be meeting her contact soon? A certain female Network agent, code-named the Swallow. It fits together, doesn't it?"

"But you said Cooper wasn't going out of town," Frank reminded her.

Nancy scowled. "Well, he didn't *say* he was."

"So what do we do about it?" asked Joe.

"We keep an eye on Cooper," Nancy said firmly. "Follow him, see what he's up to."

Frank pointed to the note in Nancy's hand. "Wait a second. If Klaus knows who the Swallow's contact is, and it *is* Bill Cooper, we'll put Bess's life in danger by following Cooper. The note said to forget about the Swallow."

Nancy looked anxiously at Frank. "Bess's life is already in danger," she said. "Besides, it's the only thing we *can* do."

"Okay," said Joe. "But let's not forget the other angle on this case: Louie's guitar. I'm still hoping it has Pritchitt's information packet in it—and maybe more precise details than we have already. I'm going to go to the Rock Spot to look for it. You two look for Cooper."

Nancy nodded. "Okay. And we'll leave messages for each other at the desk, the way we planned before."

"You'd better take the car," Frank said to his brother, then had second thoughts. "And if something happens to it this time—"

"Don't even *think* about it," Joe said. "I'll be careful, don't worry."

"There you all are," said a familiar voice. "I've been looking for you."

Frank looked up into Beau's round face. Before he could say hello, Nancy jumped in.

"Any luck?" she asked.

Frank didn't think he had ever seen Nancy so uneasy during a case. But then again, her best friend's life was at stake.

Beau shook his head. "Not a bit," he said. "No hotel has a Tracy Brandt listed, though they all have guests who look like her."

"Well, thanks anyway," Frank told him. He told Beau about Pritchitt's truck, but decided not to mention the warning note from Klaus.

Worry was clearly etched on Beau's face. "What can I do now?" he asked.

There would be no talking him out of joining them, Frank saw. He was too determined. With a quick look at Nancy, Frank said, "Come on, Beau. You can join us for a dinner cruise on a steamboat."

It was ten minutes after ten when Joe checked his watch. From where he hid, in a shadowy corner of the parking lot, he could see the front doors of the Pyramid without being seen. The car was parked behind some Dumpsters, where it wasn't noticeable. He'd been standing watch for almost forty-five minutes, but the restaurant was still open.

The stainless steel side of the Pyramid shone a ghostly white in the moonlight. Joe spotted movement at the entrance to the complex and ducked behind a post deep in the shadows.

The doors opened and several people came out. Among them Joe recognized Spence Burbank and Jeff Eliot. Joe looked at his watch. Ten-fifteen—another bad night for business.

He darted out from behind the post and made his way to the back of the huge building. There he found the bathroom window Nancy had told him about.

Good, it's still unlocked, he thought, silently thanking Nancy. No one had discovered that she had taken the latch that locked it. Opening the window as quietly as possible, he pulled himself up and through the opening.

At first it was so dark that Joe couldn't see his

hand in front of his face. He fumbled along the wall until he found a door. He opened it and stepped quietly through.

A faint red glow filtered into the restaurant from the security lights in the hallway. Joe looked around and saw that he was at the rear of the Rock Spot. Across the room were the glass doors that opened into the rest of the Pyramid complex. Briefly Joe wondered if he should worry about a security guard, but he couldn't see one.

Letting his eyes adjust to the shadows, Joe walked cautiously along the back wall until he came to the kitchen door. Figuring that the supply room had to be near the kitchen, he pushed the door open.

The stainless steel kitchen counters gleamed, even in semidarkness. They looked spotless—probably because they hadn't been used tonight, Joe told himself. He wove through dangling pots and pans and past the countertops.

Joe found a locked door on the left rear wall. His adrenaline began pumping. It had to be the storage closet. The lock would be no problem—inside doors rarely had sturdy locks. From his back pocket he pulled a slender file and a penlight, which he flicked on.

He tinkered with the lock until he heard it click, and then pushed the door open. It was pitch-black inside.

His penlight revealed that the supply room was completely full. Tablecloths and napkins were stacked against the wall. Plates were piled on a heavy table. Boxes of forks and knives, extra candles, and spare menus lay on industrial shelving. The only thing Joe didn't see was a guitar.

Stepping deeper into the closet, he shone the light methodically from left to right, front to back. In the far corner he spotted some sheets of cardboard. Large boxes had been folded flat and leaned against the wall.

Joe shone the light behind the cardboard, and there he found what he was looking for. The blue finish on the electric guitar glistened in the penlight's beam. A shadow of the graceful curve of the instrument fell on the wall beyond.

His pulse racing, Joe took the guitar out. He laid the penlight on the table and shook the instrument lightly. Something inside rattled.

Joe turned it upside down and shook again. Whatever was inside banged around and finally hit the strings of the guitar with a soft vibrating sound. Carefully Joe slipped it out.

It was a smudged, wrinkled envelope. Fighting an impulse to frantically rip it open, Joe slid a finger carefully under the flap to loosen the seal. Then he shook the contents of the envelope onto his hand—a torn scrap of lined notebook paper and a color photograph.

Joe looked at the note first. On it were the same words Nancy and Frank had gotten from the pad at Hank Pritchitt's house, which told of the midnight meeting at the Gulf of Mexico. Joe flipped the sheet over, looking for something more specific, but found nothing.

Picking up the light, Joe studied the photograph. He let out a low whistle when he saw that Bill Cooper's face was circled. "So Cooper *was* the Swallow's contact," he whispered to himself.

Suddenly the overhead light blinked on. Joe whipped around, dropping both the photo and note.

His gaze traveled upward, from the white shoes, to the elegant white slacks, and straight into the muzzle of a double-barreled shotgun.

"I thought I saw a rat lurking in the parking lot," Jeff Eliot growled. Joe noticed his voice had lost all of its earlier phony politeness. "So I decided to come back and make sure the restaurant wasn't infested."

Joe swallowed hard. I might as well tough it out, he thought. "I'm onto you," he told Jeff Eliot. "You might as well let me go."

"Is that so?" Jeff gave him an icy smile. "It appears to me I've come across a burglar in my restaurant. I don't think I'd have a hard time convincing the police I shot you in self-defense after surprising you in the middle of a robbery."

"My friends know I'm here," Joe said. "And they know why."

"Sure they do. Many burglars work in teams."

Joe felt his stomach sink. It was obvious that Jeff Eliot wasn't falling for his bluff.

"And as for that guitar there," Jeff continued,

"it's about to find a new home. I was saving it for sentimental reasons, but it's become a bit of a bother. I suppose I'll have to send it on a trip down the river."

Joe's anger exploded. "You stole the guitar," he spat out. "You called Beau Davis out to Sun Studios to set him up, then stole Louie's guitar. You also tried to burn Left-Hand Louie's down by setting a fire in that Dumpster."

"Between you and me," Jeff said quietly, "that's true. And it's just the beginning. You see, it's very important to me that Louie's place goes out of business. My own little venture here is not doing as well as I'd hoped. But I refuse to fail because of the competition from some greasy little hamburger joint. Once I get rid of that restaurant, people will flock to the Rock Spot. There'll be lines out the door."

Joe couldn't believe what he heard. "People will never flock to a lousy place like this." He sneered. "You're fooling yourself."

Jeff Eliot raised the shotgun, and Joe's breath caught in his throat. "If I am," Eliot said calmly, sighting down the barrel, "that's my right. And I'm about to show you why." His hand tensed with the movement of his trigger finger.

Joe snatched up a plate and whipped it like a Frisbee toward Jeff Eliot. A look of panic flitted across the restaurant owner's face. He lifted the shotgun to fend off the plate.

Joe made a flying leap, knocking into Eliot

183

with all of his strength. The two of them tumbled into the kitchen.

Breaking free of Eliot, Joe leapt to his feet and ran for the door. He could hear the man behind him, struggling to get up. Joe had to get through the kitchen door before Jeff could aim the gun.

From five feet away Joe dived forward, hitting the swinging doors and tumbling into the dining room. Then he dashed through the tables, heading for the glass doors that led into the Pyramid. It was his best chance. Once he made it out of the restaurant, he could look for an emergency exit.

The sound of doors clattering behind him told Joe that Eliot was now in the room. Joe glanced back and saw Jeff leveling the gun at him.

Joe dived to the floor as the gun roared. The buckshot hit the glass doors, shattering them. Jumping up, Joe ran through the opening and into the hall of the Pyramid. He looked around frantically for a security guard but didn't see one. How could they not have a security guard in a big place like this? he thought, panicked. But there was no time to linger over the question.

A glowing panel on a wall seemed to indicate a possible exit. Joe dashed for it but found it wasn't an exit. It was one of the elevators.

He whipped around and saw Jeff Eliot enter the hallway. Joe jabbed the elevator call button, glancing over his shoulder at Eliot again. Jeff was running forward, raising the gun. The elevator doors were still shut.

Seeing that the doors were slightly recessed, Joe threw himself against them as the gun roared again. A spray of holes appeared on the wall—right where Joe had stood a second before!

Suddenly the doors opened, and Joe fell backward into the elevator. Steadying himself, he hit the up button. His heart was pounding. He hit the button again, but the elevator didn't start up right away. Waiting for it to move, Joe saw the parking lot outside through the glass walls of the elevator.

Then Joe noticed a trapdoor on the ceiling. He leapt up and knocked the door open. Then, grabbing the frame, he pulled himself onto the elevator roof and outside.

He was startled when he heard the sound of the closing elevator doors being jammed. Looking through the trapdoor, Joe saw Jeff Eliot's face sneering up at him through the opening.

Panting from exertion, Joe looked to the ground below. The jump looked possible, maybe ten feet down. Just as Joe was gearing himself up, though, the elevator lurched into motion.

The elevator car gained speed quickly. Within seconds Joe realized that the jump was no longer possible as he watched the ground appear farther and farther away. The building's outer surface of corrugated stainless steel offered no handholds.

Eliot swung the shotgun up and aimed. Joe threw himself backward as the gun went off. He avoided the buckshot, but the force of the move sent him sprawling to the edge of the elevator's roof.

For an aching moment he tried to catch his balance, but it was no good. He slipped off the roof, hit the side of the elevator track, and started falling.

As he tumbled past the glass sides of the elevator he saw Jeff leering at him. Then he dropped past the bottom of the elevator, gathering speed.

Chapter

Twenty

JOE FELT HIMSELF slam into something hard. He tumbled down the sloping side of the Pyramid, moving so fast he couldn't tell which way was up.

Flailing desperately, Joe tried to grab something, anything, on the wall. His fingers scraped twice on metal without catching hold. Then he clamped on to a bar of some sort. The jar of his halt nearly tore his body loose from his arm. Joe gasped for air, dangling on the side of the elevator track.

He now saw that he hung from one of the twin rails for the elevator. It would be a long descent, six or seven floors.

Above him, he saw that the elevator had

reached the top of the Pyramid. Soon it would start back down. There was no way he could make it to the ground before the elevator over- took him. He had to get out of the car's path or be crushed.

Joe groped along the corner of the Pyramid for a handhold. There was a small ridge in the metal siding near the corner rail. If he got a slight grip on it—no, it wasn't enough of a hold to take his whole weight. But Joe found that if he rested his feet on the slanted wall, his running shoes could get a bit of traction on the corrugated steel.

Trying not to think of the deadly drop, Joe eased away from the elevator track, gripping the metal ridge as best as he could and planting his running shoes against the wall. Joe's fingers screamed in agony, but he held tight. He had to wait for the car to pass by, and when it did, he would jump onto the top of it.

The wall sloped away from the track beyond the metal ridge, and Joe flattened himself against the Pyramid's side. Jeff Eliot might not even see him. If Eliot thought he'd fallen to his death, he wouldn't spend any time looking for him.

Joe felt a gentle push of air as the car passed by. He stiffened, half expecting to hear another shot- gun blast. But none came.

As soon as the elevator had passed, Joe pulled his body back into the track. Sliding down the rail, Joe reached the top of the elevator car. Keeping as far from the trapdoor as possible so

Jeff Eliot couldn't see him, Joe relaxed for the ride down. This wasn't quite what I had in mind, Joe thought, when I told Nancy I wanted to ride this thing.

The elevator reached bottom. Joe was about to jump off onto the ground when he heard the door opening below. Voices rose through the open trapdoor. Someone was talking to Jeff Eliot. Who else would be here at this time of night? Joe wondered.

"Don't hurt me!" Joe heard Eliot cry.

Something heavy clattered to the floor, and Joe figured it was Jeff Eliot's shotgun. Then came the sounds of footsteps as Eliot and the other person stepped out of the car and into the Pyramid. Finally the door closed.

Cautiously Joe peered down through the trapdoor and saw with relief that the car was empty. He jumped down. Putting his ear to the crack in the elevator door, he listened for the sound of people on the other side. There was no noise. Joe hit the button that opened the door and slipped into the hall.

Jeff Eliot was just disappearing into the restaurant. Joe couldn't believe who was with him. Holding a gun on Eliot was the blond-haired operative with the scar.

A chill ran down Joe's spine. How could the man have known to come here unless he had been following Joe? And did that mean there were also tails on Frank and Nancy?

Joe crept forward, inching his way up to the shattered glass door of the restaurant. Across the room he saw Jeff and the operative enter the kitchen, no doubt heading for the storage closet—and the photo and note. Joe could kick himself for not having grabbed them. But he'd had other things on his mind—such as staying alive.

Joe dashed across the room and silently pushed open the kitchen door. Sure enough, the door to the storage closet was open and the light was on. A cord from the kitchen telephone stretched into the room as well.

"Cooper's the one we want," came the spy's icy voice. Joe figured he had to be talking to someone on the phone, probably Klaus. "Put the girl somewhere on his riverboat. Somewhere lethal."

Joe's mouth fell open. The girl had to be Bess! He needed to warn Nancy and Frank immediately.

"Now for *you*," the agent said after he hung up. Joe heard a babbled protest from Jeff Eliot, then a meaty *thunk* as the restaurant owner was knocked out.

Joe tiptoed out of the kitchen, through the dining room, and into the bathroom. The window was still open, and he hoisted himself up and dived through it.

Staying close to the side of the Pyramid, Joe decided to wait for the spy to leave before he ran to the car. Five minutes went by before the blond man got into his sedan and drove off, apparently not seeing Joe or his car.

Joe had planned to drive to the Peabody and leave a message and then head out to the riverboat landing to look for Nancy and Frank. But then Joe spotted a pay phone next to the parking lot. First he called the hotel and left a message for the others. Then he called the police and told them about Jeff Eliot.

Then he ran for the car.

At last, Nancy thought, we're getting somewhere.

She, Frank, and Beau had trailed Bill Cooper all evening. First they'd taken the dinner cruise on his boat. The river captain had seemed delighted that they'd joined him. He even inquired after Bess, sending his condolences when Nancy told him she wasn't feeling well.

When the boat had docked at nine-thirty, the three teenagers had pretended to leave. Instead, they hid while Cooper and his crew closed things down, then trailed him on foot to a small restaurant nearby, where he had a late dinner.

After his meal Bill Cooper headed for the boat again, and the three teenagers followed him there. They found a car in the marina's parking lot to hide behind and watched Cooper go aboard. He undid ropes, tossing them ashore, until there were only two lines holding the boat to the dock. Then he went up to the cabin on the top deck.

"Looks like he's getting ready to go out again." Frank checked his watch. "It's a quarter to midnight. How can he possibly take the riverboat all the way to the Gulf of Mexico in fifteen minutes?"

Beau shook his head. "I don't think he'd make it down to the gulf before Saturday in that thing."

Suddenly, out the corner of her eye, Nancy saw something. "Frank, look," she said in a low voice, pointing across the parking lot.

A figure was running toward them.

"It's Joe!" Frank darted out from behind the car and ran over to his brother. A moment later the two of them returned to the hiding place.

"Cooper's the one," said Joe. He was still panting from his run. "And Bess is tied up somewhere on his boat. 'Somewhere lethal' is what I heard that guy with the blond crew cut say."

Nancy's heart leapt into her throat. "Cooper is about to start up the boat. We've got to stop him!" she said in a frantic whisper.

"Look," Frank told her. "Cooper's getting *off* the boat."

Nancy let out a sigh of relief. Cooper was walking down the gangplank. He went to the front of the boat and stooped over next to a large mooring. There he untied a rope, much smaller than the ones holding the riverboat.

He stepped off the dock. From the gentle up-and-down motion of his body, Nancy guessed that he was standing in a small boat.

"What's going on?" Joe whispered.

Cooper started rowing into the river, heading toward Mud Island.

Suddenly it hit Nancy. "Of course!" She gasped. "We've missed it all along!"

Frank, Joe, and Beau looked at her blankly.

"Cooper's not heading to the *actual* Gulf of Mexico," Nancy explained excitedly. "Remember the model of the Mississippi River over there? It lets out into a swimming pool at the base of the island. *That's* the Gulf of Mexico."

Joe smacked his forehead. "You're right!"

"Which means the meeting is about to happen," Frank added eagerly. "We've got them."

"Uh-oh," muttered Beau, staring out over the water. "Don't mean to spoil your party, but take a look over there."

Darkness made it hard to see. Nancy could barely distinguish a few shadowy forms moving on the island. Moonlight glinted off metal. Klaus's operatives had arrived—with guns!

"We've got to get over there," Nancy said urgently. "But we also have to find Bess."

"I'll get Bess," Beau offered. From the determined look on his face, Nancy knew he wouldn't take no for an answer.

"You shouldn't go alone," Joe warned Beau. "I'll come with you."

Nancy was torn. Bess was in grave danger on the riverboat. But Klaus would surely kill the Swallow and Cooper if he caught them. She looked at Frank. "I guess you and I had better head for the island."

In a matter of seconds they ran to the Mud Island ticket booth and vaulted over the turnstiles.

Nancy pointed to a sign. "This way to the walkway," she said in a low voice. She ran up a set of concrete stairs, hearing Frank's running shoes pounding right behind her.

As she rounded the corner at the top of the stairs, Nancy came to a halt. Her heart sank. The covered walkway stretched before them, a stroll of a few hundred yards to the island. Right in front of it, however, was a big iron gate. It went all the way to the ceiling, preventing them from climbing over.

She rattled the gate. "It even has one of those high-tech locks. No way to pick it."

"I've got another idea," said Frank. Turning on his heel, he started back down the stairs. Nancy ran after him. By the time she got to the bottom of the stairs, Frank stood next to a door and was shoving the blade of a pocketknife into the crack between the door and its frame. On the door were painted the words *Tramway Control—Private.*

The door swung open just as Nancy reached him, and the two of them ran inside.

Frank headed for the control room. "Quick, go to the tram," he called. "I'm going to start it up."

Nancy ran over to the tram. It was about the size of a bus, with large windows all the way around. A couple of vertical shafts connected it to a rail above. The rail ran underneath the walkway they had just tried to cross.

The tram engines ground to life, and the door in front of Nancy slid open. Frank ran up beside her. "Let's go," he said, grinning.

Inside the doors there was a small control panel. Frank hit the Door Close button, and then hit one labeled To Island. Soon the tram lurched forward.

"I wouldn't call this the least conspicuous way to reach the island," Nancy said.

Frank shrugged. "It's the only way we've got right now." He took a deep breath. "Besides, Klaus and company should be busy trying to catch Cooper. Let's just hope he keeps them distracted."

"Right." Looking down, Nancy saw the river fifty feet below, shimmering in the moonlight. She could see Cooper's boat, halfway between the mainland and the island.

Nancy frowned. He had stopped rowing. What was wrong?

She shifted her gaze to the island itself. Now that she and Frank were closer to it, they had a clearer view. But what Nancy saw sickened her.

Tracy Brandt's pale face grinned in a shaft of moonlight. She stood on Mud Island, pointing straight at the tram. Apparently, Cooper's arrival hadn't distracted her. Nancy watched in horror as one of the operatives nodded his head and started running toward the tramway platform.

"We've got trouble, Frank!" Nancy cried.

The man reached the platform. He looked around for a moment, then found a thick metal bar. The tram was pulled by a long cable, which wrapped around a large wheel. The operative jammed the metal bar through the spokes of the wheel.

As the bar hit the concrete housing, the tram car stopped abruptly. Nancy and Frank were both thrown to the floor. Quickly they both scrambled to their feet.

"We're stuck!" Frank pounded the control panel. "Now there's no way we can keep Klaus from nailing the Swallow."

Nancy's stomach lurched as another thought occurred to her. "And not only that," she said, "we're sitting targets!"

Chapter

Twenty-One

WAIT A MINUTE," Nancy suddenly said to Frank. "We're not trapped yet." She went to the control panel and hit the Door Open button. Nothing happened. "Frank, help me force open the doors."

"Nancy, are you crazy? We're fifty feet up in the air. We can't jump down to the river."

"No—but we can climb up to the rail."

Frank stared at her for a moment. "You're right," he said at last. "That's our only hope."

The double doors of the tram car met in a rubber seal. Together, Nancy and Frank worked their fingers into the rubber and started pulling.

The doors resisted, but Nancy and Frank kept tearing at them. Finally they heard the sound of grinding machinery. With a sudden lurch the doors gave way and slid open.

"You first," Frank said. "I'll hold the doors open and boost you up."

Frank braced his feet between the doors. Nancy looked down and saw there was nothing between them and the water far below. Frank was right. A drop from this height would kill.

Standing on her toes, she reached up and groped for a hold. The roof was smooth—it was hard to keep her grip. Then Frank cradled her foot in his two hands and lifted her. Gritting her teeth, Nancy hauled with all her might. Seconds later she was on the roof.

"Made it!" she whispered to Frank.

While Frank climbed up, Nancy scoped out the island. They'd gotten one lucky break—the man who'd jammed the tram had joined the others on the shore. Nancy smiled grimly. *He thinks we're still trapped.*

Bill Cooper had turned around in his boat to face Tracy Brandt. From across the water Nancy could hear them shouting to each other.

"I don't think you can outrow a bullet!" Brandt shouted. "And we have kidnapped a girl. If you and the Swallow make an attempt to get away, the girl will die, and it will be your doing."

Nancy climbed a ladder up one of the car

shafts to the tram rail. She had to get to the island—fast!

Next came the hard part. Wrapping her hands around the rail, she worked them slowly away from the car.

"Go for it," Frank whispered.

Nancy swung her body forward, dangling over the water below. With a deep breath she took all her weight on her left hand, swinging her right forward along the rail. She grabbed hold again, about a foot ahead.

Frank whispered, "I'm right behind you."

She swung her left hand forward, trying to move as fast as possible. Her arms already ached from holding her body up. She grabbed for the next section of rail ahead.

Nancy fought her fatigue to increase the speed of her hand-over-hand progress. Every breath felt as if she were sucking flames. But the island wasn't far now.

Behind her she could hear Frank panting. They had to keep going. With agonizing slowness the tramway station came closer.

As Nancy finally dropped onto the landing, her knees buckled and she collapsed in a heap. She had made it!

Frank dropped down next to Nancy, and they both sat still for a moment, gasping for breath. But Nancy couldn't ignore the voices below.

"I want to see Klaus," Cooper demanded.

Tracy Brandt laughed wickedly. *"I'm* Klaus, you fool."

Nancy was so shocked, she almost cried out. She and Frank stared at each other in disbelief.

Bill Cooper sounded shocked, too. "You—you're the woman who came over to me at the Peabody. Asking me all those questions about my plans. Why, you—"

Tracy Brandt's evil laugh cut him off. "You thought your little meeting tonight was safe. You were clever—but not clever enough."

"But how—" Cooper's voice sounded confused.

"You should have been more wary of tourists asking simple questions about the Gulf of Mexico. Telling me about the scale model here on Mud Island was most helpful."

"The Swallow has made it this far, and she's not about to be caught," came Cooper's voice.

So Tracy Brandt is Klaus, Nancy thought. And she hasn't gotten to the Swallow yet.

"And I'm not about to hand her over," Cooper went on. "I'll die if I have to." Brave words, Nancy thought, but she heard a waver in his voice.

"Tsk, tsk," came Tracy Brandt's icy reply. "We've worked so hard to avoid silly scenes like this. Why do you think we went to the trouble of sneaking poor Pritchitt into the hotel, killing him where everyone would find him? As a warning, of course. We dropped a hotel tray on one of those boy scouts who came hunting for your precious Swallow—and we kidnapped the girl. You could save her life, you know." Brandt paused, and when Cooper didn't reply, she said, "You're willing to let the girl die, too?"

Nancy couldn't believe the cold-blooded ruthlessness in Brandt's voice.

Frank took a few deep breaths, tapped Nancy on the shoulder, then whispered, "Ready to go?"

Keeping as much to the shadows as they could, the two of them tucked into crouches and made their way down the concrete steps. They reached the ground and ran quickly and silently, circling around behind Brandt and her two men.

Nancy could see that both of the agents aimed machine guns. Tracy Brandt had a pistol but held it loosely. With her thugs nearby, Nancy thought, she didn't need the gun.

A low cement wall ran to within ten feet of Brandt's position. Nancy and Frank worked their way along the far side, keeping their heads down.

"There's no reason to kill the girl," Cooper said desperately. "She's innocent. Let her go."

"Innocent?" Tracy Brandt laughed. "She knows too much. And so do her friends. The girl lives only as long as she is useful to me."

Nancy gasped and then held her hand over her mouth, afraid she might cry out in fear and anger. She wanted to leap over the wall and fling herself on Tracy Brandt—or Klaus. Frank grabbed Nancy's arm, and she snapped back to reality.

They were trapped here, ten feet away from Brandt and her men. As long as Bess was a captive, there was nothing they could do but watch.

"Follow me," Joe instructed Beau.

They had paused in the shadow of a huge piling by the dock.

"The boat's dark," Joe whispered. "But there may be a guard on it. We'll have to be careful."

He looked furtively around, then sprinted up the gangway and onto the lower deck, Beau right behind him. Again Joe paused, listening.

Beau whispered, "Somewhere . . . somewhere lethal. It has to be a place with moving parts."

"Like the engine room," Joe said. "I'll check down there. You look around on the deck. Whistle if you find anything."

In the dark it was hard for Joe to find his way among the smokestacks, ducts, and storage bins, but he made it into the cabin. It was deathly quiet, yet he had the eerie sensation that he and Beau weren't alone.

His running shoes squeaked loudly on the steep metal stairs leading down from the cabin to the engine room. At the foot of the stairs he blinked, trying to pierce the blackness. He could hear a low pounding as the engines built up pressure. Where in this gloom could he find Bess?

"Joe!" Beau's voice was frantic. "Come quick!"

Joe bolted up the stairs and back out onto the deck. He saw Beau waving frantically from the stern of the boat. Joe was there in a flash.

"Look!" Beau pointed down behind the railing at the paddle wheel.

The shadow of the boat fell over the wheel, so Joe found himself peering into darkness again.

He heard a muffled whimper and then made out a shape. It was Bess, bound and gagged—and tied to one of the blades of the paddle wheel!

Chapter

Twenty-Two

J OE TURNED TO BEAU. "Well? What are we waiting for?" He leapt over the rail and began scrambling over the paddle wheel. The wheel was wet and slippery, and several times Joe almost slid into the water. At last they reached the paddle where Bess was tied.

Her eyes were big in the darkness, until Joe said, "It's okay, Bess. It's me, Joe, and Beau."

"You all right?" Beau asked as he pulled the gag off her.

Bess's voice was a little shaky, but she managed a laugh. "I—I'm glad you finally turned up. It's not polite to ditch your date, you know."

Both Beau and Joe had pocketknives, and they went to work on the rope.

"We've got to hurry," Joe said. "Nancy and Frank may need us on Mud Island."

Still crouching under the wall, Frank and Nancy sneaked a look over the top to where Tracy Brandt and her two henchmen stood.

"I'm getting tired of this!" Brandt raised her gun and pointed it at Cooper. "The Swallow is here somewhere, and you're going to tell me where. We'll find her anyway, but you're going to make it easy for us—and easy on yourself."

Nancy saw Bill Cooper's face go pale, but he remained silent.

Brandt raised her voice. "Swallow!" she shouted. "Show yourself now, or I'll put a bullet in Cooper's brain!"

A tense silence hung in the air.

Suddenly the deep, throbbing sound of an engine shattered the air. It came from the direction of the mainland. Nancy could feel Frank tensing beside her.

Looking behind Cooper, Nancy spotted a Delta Duck cutting through the water. As it roared closer, Nancy made out three figures at the helm—Joe, Beau, and Bess.

Frank and Nancy both exchanged a glance and scrambled onto the top of the cement wall.

"Now!" Nancy shouted, hearing Frank shout the same thing.

Frank jumped off the wall and onto the blond operative, while Nancy dived for Tracy Brandt. Brandt let out a surprised grunt and aimed her pistol at Nancy as she caught the spy around the waist. Nancy struggled for the pistol, her tired arms burning as Brandt tried to turn it toward her.

"You're crazy!" Tracy Brandt spat between clenched teeth. "And soon you'll be dead!"

"That's what you think," Nancy countered. She twisted Brandt's arm at the wrist, loosening the woman's grip. Then Nancy shook Brandt's arm, and the pistol fell to the ground.

Tracy Brandt screamed with fury, evil burning in her eyes. But she froze when Nancy covered her with the gun.

Frank had the blond spy in an armlock. He had gotten the machine gun and was trying to point it at Tracy Brandt's other agent. It wasn't easy—not with the scar-faced blond man still struggling.

The dark-haired operative looked panic-stricken, unable to choose a target for his machine gun. Finally his face hardened, and he aimed, ready to cut down Frank—*and* his comrade.

Before he could pull the trigger, though, a rock came flying from out of the darkness. It landed with a dull thud right on the dark man's forehead. He went down, his gun clattering, just as Frank finally subdued the other man.

The Delta Duck's engine roared louder and louder as it drew closer. Now it reached the island and drove right up onto the land.

Joe leapt from the vehicle, ran over to the dark-haired operative, and scooped up the loose machine gun. "Hey, it was nice of you to loan this to me." He called up to the two in the Delta Duck. "Beau, get that rope in there, will you?"

Beau came with the rope, and Bess jumped off the Duck. Her hair was tangled and her face was dirty, but Nancy was never so happy to see her.

"Thank goodness you're all right!" Nancy cried, running toward her. "I was so scared for you!"

The two friends threw their arms around each other in a big hug.

Bess told her about being tied to the paddle wheel. "The moment it started turning, I'd have been smacked into the water and drowned!" Her big blue eyes filled with tears.

Nancy gasped. Giving her friend an extra tight squeeze, she said, "It's over, Bess! You're safe now."

Nancy's attention was diverted by the sound of a boat scraping onto land. It was Bill Cooper. In the excitement she had forgotten about him. He climbed out of his dinghy and pulled it ashore.

"Captain Cooper," Nancy called, going over to him. "I guess everything turned out all right."

Cooper looked up with a grin. "So I see," he said, nodding to where Tracy Brandt and her two operatives were tied up next to the Delta Duck. "And I'm about as happy as I could ever be."

He looked past Nancy, into the darkness and shadows of the island. "Madeline," he called. "You can come out now."

Madeline? Nancy thought, then recalled who she was. In the excitement of seeing Bess again she'd forgotten all about Cooper's midnight meeting with the Swallow.

Everyone stared as a woman stepped out from behind a darkened refreshment stand. She was dressed in jeans and a black T-shirt. Her black hair cascaded over her shoulders, framing a pale face that glowed even in the muted moonlight. Looking at her, Nancy could understand why Bill Cooper would have waited a long time to be together with her again.

Cooper ran to Madeline and caught her in a fierce hug. She threw her arms around him, burying her face in his shoulder. They held each other for a long time.

Finally Madeline stepped back and looked at the group around her and Bill Cooper. "I guess I should be thanking all of you."

"Hey, Frank should be thanking you," Joe said. "I saw the way you beaned that last gunman with a rock."

Nancy just grinned, happy to see the couple reunited. They were obviously deeply in love. Walking over to Madeline, she held out her hand. "I'm Nancy Drew," she said.

Madeline shook her hand. "Madeline Swift."

Frank and Joe came up beside Nancy. Joe introduced himself and Frank to Madeline.

"We're working for the Network," Frank added quietly.

Madeline's eyes widened with shock. She gave Cooper a despairing look.

Then she turned back to Joe and Frank and said sadly, "I guess that means that you're going to turn me in."

Frank didn't like being the one to tell Madeline that she wasn't quite free of her responsibilities as a spy. "The Network needs to talk to you," Frank said gently. "The information you have is very valuable to them."

"It won't take long," Joe added. "And then you can go on with your life."

Nancy had been so happy to see the couple reunited that she'd almost forgotten about the Swallow's information. Her curiosity made her ask, "Could you tell us your story, Madeline?"

It was Bill Cooper who stepped forward. "I'll tell it," he said quietly. "Most of this mess is my fault anyway." He stood silent for a moment, working his jaw. "I met Madeline three years ago, by pure accident.

"I was in Germany for a conference," he said, addressing the group as a whole. "Believe it or not, it was about Mark Twain. Being a riverboat captain, I'm also something of a Mark Twain scholar, since he wrote about riverboats. Anyway, Mr. Twain has a big following in Germany, and so they sponsored my trip over there to give a lecture. I was excited to go."

Cooper nodded toward Madeline. Nancy noticed he took every opportunity to shoot her loving glances. "Madeline came to these conferences," he continued. "If you're from the Network, you know she was trapped in East Germany. She had assumed the identity of an East German government employee. After Grady was murdered, Madeline had to rely on this identity for her livelihood. Being a government worker, she wasn't allowed to leave the country."

"Grady was my only contact and—things were bad." Madeline shuddered. "Klaus was searching all over for me, so I didn't dare call attention to myself. My job involved the international conferences, so at least sometimes I could hear English spoken."

Cooper gave her a sad smile and picked up the story. "So we met. I couldn't do anything about getting her out, but I sure was happy to give her a little company. What can I say? I fell in love with Madeline the second I saw her. I couldn't believe it, but she fell in love with me, too. We came to trust each other completely. Madeline told me all about her past.

"When I had to leave the country, I thought I'd never see her again." A sad look came into his eyes, as if he were reliving his despair. "But then

Madeline told me she thought the Berlin Wall would be coming down soon and that she'd be able to come home."

Nancy nodded. So far their story fit what she and the Hardys already knew.

"She was right about the Wall," Cooper went on. "And she sent me a letter telling me when she was coming home. All we wanted was to be together again. But there was a traitor loose in the Network—a double agent who was working for Klaus. Nobody over here really believed he existed, but Madeline knew who he was."

He nodded toward Brandt. "With Germany being reunited, Klaus was out of a job. So she decided to go free-lance. After all, she still had a blackmailed Network double agent on her string. A lot of countries would like that kind of information pipeline. The only problem was that Madeline knew who the agent was.

"Madeline didn't care about that, though," Cooper went on. "After the trouble she had gone through for the Network, she just wanted to disappear somewhere in the United States and live out her life as a civilian."

A look of disappointment came over his face. Disappointment, Nancy thought, with himself.

"But I couldn't keep quiet about it. I told a friend who I thought could help us—Hank Pritchitt. Instead, Pritchitt decided to help himself by giving us away. He turned right around and tried to sell his information to the Network. I could have killed him for it." With a grim look he added, "But I didn't have to. Klaus did it for me."

Madeline straightened her shoulders and said, "I was afraid to contact the Network myself, but I can see you can be trusted. I'll be happy to talk to your man at the Network. I'd like to see Klaus's double agent picked up as soon as possible."

Frank grinned at her. "I'm sure the Network will appreciate that. And I hope they won't detain you long."

Madeline shook her head soberly. "Klaus's double agent has a long history of treachery. I want to make sure the Network learns all of it, and about Klaus's remaining operations."

Joe grinned. "All right! Let's hear it for the good guys!"

The next day Nancy, Bess, the Hardys, and Beau were all sitting around a table in the Rendezvous. In front of each of them was a huge rack of ribs, cooked to perfection and coated with the restaurant's famous barbecue sauce. Festive decorations lined the walls, giving the restaurant a carnival atmosphere.

Nancy noted that the Hardys were both a little bleary-eyed. That wasn't surprising. After all, they had been up most of the night.

Frank continued to fill Beau in on the case. "So we called the Gray Man. Woke him up at one in the morning and told him we had Klaus tied up in front of us. He made some calls, and Network agents showed up at Mud Island within an hour. They're holed up with Madeline right now, debriefing her."

"So Tracy Brandt is Klaus," Beau said. "And she was right under your noses all along."

"I had my suspicions about her," Nancy said, "but no real evidence."

"What happened to the money?" Bess asked. She looked at Nancy with a wry grin and added, "I sure could have a good time at the malls with that bundle of cash."

"We got it back," Joe said. "Or at least, the Network got it back. With a photograph of Brandt, or Klaus, I should say, it was easy to find out which hotel she was staying at. She'd come up with another name to register under. We found the money along with all the bugging equipment she was using to listen in on us."

"And that's not all," said Frank. "There are prints all over Hank Pritchitt's pickup truck, and they match Klaus's men's prints. I guess they were so sure they wouldn't get caught that they didn't bother to wipe the truck clean."

"Poor Hank," Beau said with sadness in his deep voice. "The guy got in over his head with this thing. But at least he didn't sell his info to Klaus."

"No, he wasn't that greedy," Joe said.

"How did Klaus know the Swallow was a

woman before you all figured it out?" Beau asked, trying to fit the pieces of the case together. "And how did she know to go to the model of the Gulf of Mexico instead of the real thing?"

"Klaus pumped Bill Cooper for information once she discovered that we thought Cooper could be the Swallow's contact," Nancy said. "Cooper told Klaus about the model of the gulf, not knowing that he was talking to a spy. And he must have mentioned that he was expecting to see Madeline after a long separation. So Klaus figured out the rest from there."

"What I still don't get," Beau said, "is how Klaus knew about your investigation in the first place. How did she know you were coming to Memphis and staying at the Peabody?"

"Grady's suspicion was on target," Frank said. "There is a double agent working in the Network who must have told Klaus about us. That's also how Klaus and her men knew to hit on Hank Pritchitt before we got to him."

"And now that we've uncovered the Swallow's identity, Madeline can reveal to the Network the identity of the double agent," Joe added.

Nancy beamed at her friends. "So I guess that means you guys are heroes with the Network now, huh?" she said to Frank and Joe.

"The Gray Man's not one for showing his appreciation," Frank said, "but he did say something about how he was grateful we didn't screw up."

Joe grinned. "And that's about as big a compliment as we've ever gotten from him."

"Terrific," Bess said. She gave everyone at the table an enthusiastic look. "So now that the case is wrapped up, that means we've got time to kill. And you know what I was wondering?"

Nancy grinned at her. "What?" she asked.

Bess clapped her hands together. "Does anyone want to see Graceland?"

"I promised I'd take you there, Bess," Beau said. "We'll go tomorrow."

"At least someone around here has a date," Joe quipped.